Disposition,

The Catalyst

a novel by

James E. Ballou

Black Rose Writing

www.blackrosewriting.com

ISBN: 978-1-61296-051-7

PUBLISHED BY BLACK ROSE WRITING

www.blackrosewriting.com

Printed in the United States of America

Disposition, The Catalyst is printed in Book Antiqua

To my sister, Caroline

Disposition,

The Catalyst

Jim Ballou

Chapter 1

The Catalyst

◊

Daren McBride took his last long slow gulp of cold beer and then planted the emptied bottle on the kitchen table in front of him, right next to the loaded Smith & Wesson revolver. He stared down at the gun, and let everything he'd been dwelling on over the last few weeks run through his brain one more time, just to make sure he really wanted to do what he had been planning to do. It was just then that he heard the knocking at the front door.

At first he tried to ignore it. Whoever was at the door would soon go away, he assumed. But the loud rapping on the door continued. It was a persistent interruption, and it became increasingly annoying to him. Why wouldn't the person just go away after so many minutes had passed without anyone answering the door? That's what any normal person would do - figure out soon enough that either no one was home, or if at home maybe in the shower, or sleeping, or unable to get to the door for whatever reason. But not this person, whoever it was at his front door right now. The knocking didn't stop.

Maybe someone, possibly a neighbor, was having some kind of an emergency he wondered, or maybe it was the landlord, here to tell him that he would need to be out of the house sometime earlier than Friday, rather than by Noon on Friday as he was previously told. Or, maybe it was just some high-pressure door-to-door salesman.

In any case, Daren decided to get up and go answer it, to satisfy his curiosity as much as to get this interruption out of his way. He would need a quiet atmosphere free of distractions where he could properly contemplate the gravity of, and prepare himself for, what he was about to do.

To his surprise, the door opened to reveal a small, very odd looking old man with long white hair and beard, dressed in ragged clothing, with a walking cane in his left hand. This had to be a homeless person, he guessed by the man's appearance.

"Daren McBride?" the man greeted him.

"Yes, I am Daren. How can I help you?"

"I am here to show you why you don't want to do what you are considering doing. We really should talk about some very important things. May I come in?"

Daren responded with a tone that revealed his suspicion, "No, I'd prefer that you didn't enter the house. I don't even know who you are or what you want. I believe we can talk just fine right here. Who are you, anyway? How did you know my name, and how would you know anything at all about what I'm considering doing? What exactly *am* I considering doing, by the way?"

"You are considering taking your own life. Oh, it's irrelevant who I am really. In your mind I'm just an old homeless man. Call me Tom if you like."

"Okay, 'Tom', what business is it of yours if I am contemplating taking my own life? Did Mr. Harrington send you here to tell me that, so that I wouldn't bloody up his kitchen and lower his property value? That selfish jerk knows full well what sort of hell my life has been lately, because he's as much a part of it as everything else. He might be expecting me to consider blowing my brains out, all right. How much does he have to pay you to come talk to me? My guess is that he only had to bribe you with a cheap bottle of wine or maybe a pack of cigarettes, am I right?"

"Well, no, that's not why I'm here. If that were the case I would have to donate any amount of payment entirely to charity, as I don't smoke or drink, and I don't need money. But I am not here on behalf of, or even to talk about your landlord. That man has his own journey. I am strictly here to show you another way."

Daren couldn't help noticing that the man's eyes were a very unusual shade of greenish blue – almost turquoise in color. He'd never seen eyes of that same color before. Everything about this little old man seemed eerily strange. He seemed to know more things than he should know.

"Another way for *what?*" Daren asked.

"Another way in which to live your life, or to die if

3

that's your choice. It has to do with how you view your world. You see, you have ordered your own reality by the disposition you've adopted. You've had quite a chip on your shoulder for some time. What you need right now is what some would call a 'catalyst', which is something that will start the re-ordering process, to change your disposition. Ultimately that will make all the difference to you."

"Listen, Mister, I don't know who you are... Okay, yeah, you said your name is Tom. But I'm pretty sure I've never even met you before, and I don't know why you think you've got any right to advise me about my attitude...or my 'disposition' - whatever. That's my own personal business, and it's not any issue for some stranger who comes around and simply says his name is Tom. Besides, I have much bigger problems than you could possibly understand, and my problems won't go away if I simply change my disposition."

The man shook his head and stated with a matter of fact bluntness, "I'm afraid I have to disagree with you about that, Daren. Your disposition makes *all* the difference in the world to you, and I will show you how if you will only allow me..."

Daren closed the door, and locked it. He wasn't in any mood for arguing, taking advice from strangers, or even talking to anyone at all. He wanted to go back into the kitchen, sit down, maybe drink one more cold beer before putting an end to the pain. He needed peace and quiet for that, and he just wanted to be left alone.

There were two bottles of beer left in the refrigerator, and somehow it seemed like a shame to drink only one before ending his life. It seemed like a waste of good beer, and he thought that maybe he should drink *all* the beer in the fridge before...

He had to smile about that, concerning himself about wasting beer while contemplating putting the loaded revolver to his temple and pulling the trigger. But he twisted the cap off of one of the bottles and sat down in his chair, thinking about how strange his discussion with the old man at the door suddenly seemed.

There was simply no possible way for that old man to know that he was preparing to shoot himself. It would almost make sense that he had peered in through a window and saw Daren sitting at the kitchen table drinking beer with that gun on the table in front of him, staring at it like he was in a trance, except that the curtains were closed. There was no way to see into the kitchen from the outside of the house. Besides, even if he were able to somehow see in, why the big concern? This wasn't the old man's problem.

All of that talk about his disposition was kind of weird, too. How would some strange little old white haired man have any knowledge whatsoever about his disposition? How could he possibly know that Daren had quite a chip on his shoulder? He concentrated for a few minutes trying to remember, but even if something seemed vaguely familiar about the man, he felt pretty sure that he had never met him before.

When the phone rang it startled him. He hadn't been expecting any calls. He almost decided against answering it, but then after the third ring he picked up the receiver. He wasn't even sure exactly why he decided to answer it.

"Daren McBride?"

"Yes. Who is this?"

"Hi Mr. McBride, my name is Sharon, and I'm the new receptionist in Dr. Richards office. He wanted me to schedule an appointment with you right away for consultation. We have your latest lab tests in already. He would like to meet with you as soon as possible, to go over the information with you."

"I'm sorry, Sharon, but that won't be necessary. I have made my decision already, and I have decided against taking any more treatment."

"I'll let him know of your position on that, but he still wants to sit down with you and explain some things in your charts. Would you be able to make it in this afternoon by chance, say at two thirty? The doctor has one opening at two thirty, if you can make it in."

Daren paused to think about it, and then finally agreed to come in. After he hung up the phone he wondered why he had allowed himself to agree to another trip to the doctor's office. It would just be a waste of time, just another distraction, and surely an unpleasant one at that. Now that he had made this appointment, he would have to keep it. He had always kept every appointment that he had ever made, always. Now he would have to take the time and go see his doctor, no matter how much he detested doing so.

Throughout his life, Daren had always dreaded visits to doctors' offices. Those kinds of experiences were always unpleasant for him, but at least he always expected the worst and tried to prepare himself for that, which seemed to help sometimes.

This time it wouldn't matter very much – anything the doctor could tell him now about his cancer would actually seem almost trivial in the face of his looming "day of reckoning". The burdens of this world, one of them being the terminal cancer he'd been suffering for almost four months, were about to be shed from his shoulders forever, and whatever matters he needed to clear up before leaving the stage could only be considered small details having very little relevance to him.

He didn't have to wait there in the front waiting room very long, not even long enough to look through the *Field & Stream* magazine he noticed on an end table, before the nurse appeared and called his name. He followed her down the hall to a room where he was directed to take a seat in one of the stuffed chairs at a large round oak table. Less than two minutes later the doctor entered the room, took a seat at the table, and opened up Daren's file containing his medical records on the table in front of them.

"I'm pleased to see that you're looking better today, Daren, How are you feeling?"

"I have my good moments and I have my bad moments I guess. What was it that you wanted to tell me about today, Doc?"

The doctor was slow with his answer. He seemed to be searching for just the right words, "The cancer is not letting go its grip on you I'm afraid. Those tests we ran last week provided us with a clearer picture of exactly what is going on inside you, but these were certainly not the results we were hoping to find. After we took those x-rays and I saw what I thought I saw, I wanted the lab to check it out before I talked to you. The cancer had spread more throughout your body before it went into remission than we knew previously, and it will come back. When it does, it will likely be much worse than before. I didn't know any easy way to tell you this, but you have the right to know the truth, and so here we are."

"Okay, so what does this mean in terms of how much longer I should have to live?" Daren seemed to ask the question casually, as if he didn't even care all that much what the answer would be. He knew he wasn't going to wait for the cancer to kill him.

"You'll have maybe four months, and possibly even a little bit longer, like maybe as much as five or six months if you take good care of yourself. And by taking care of yourself I mean having only one beer a day instead of a six-pack, and drinking fewer cups of coffee than you might be used to drinking each morning. I mean getting to bed at a decent hour each night, probably at least an hour or two earlier than you might now normally go to bed, and avoid strenuous physical work as much as you possibly can, although a very modest amount of exercise should actually help you. Eat regular, well-balanced healthy meals, preferably three a day. You did tell me that you've already quit smoking, so I won't go there anymore. Take proper care of your body and it might fight this thing better than it otherwise could. Changing your lifestyle only slightly can make a huge difference. And of course, I recommend that you continue with the treatment for now. Say what you will about this cancer treatment, but what you are receiving is considerably better than what they had even twenty or thirty years ago."

"Whatever caused this cancer that's eating me up inside - my years of smoking I guess, like you said, but it has sealed my fate, isn't that right, Doc? Even with the best treatment available today, I'll still be dead inside of six months. Isn't it a shame how something as enjoyable as cigarettes can cause this kind of hell in someone's existence? Do you think it's at least *possible* that there could be some other cause?"

"Well, those of us who work in the various fields of medicine have our own ideas about these things, and of course our individual opinions aren't always in total agreement, but I think we all pretty much agree that there are certain toxins in our environment, man-made or 'synthetic' chemicals usually, that act as a kind of catalyst for a lot of these increasingly common diseases and cancers.

"I do still believe tobacco is the most likely culprit in your case, just as I've said. But cures for certain types of cancer are actually being developed now, though. Amazing progress is being made all the time, and I am very encouraged by that."

There was that word again – *catalyst*. How unlikely this was, Daren thought, to hear the same relatively uncommon word spoken twice in the same day, by two different people. Was there some kind of message that he was supposed to read into any of this somewhere? He tried to dismiss that thought as naively hopeful. But there it was as plain as day, that fundamental reality of science that everything that happens is caused by something, and there was this nagging thought in the back of his mind about this whole cause-and-effect process that just

9

wouldn't go away. He couldn't stop thinking about what that little old strange white haired man, Tom, told him earlier.

"Is there such a thing do you think," Daren paused before continuing, "such a thing as some type of psychological, or like a negative energy in someone's attitude that can actually bring about certain illnesses like cancers? Could negative emotional energy in this sense act like a toxic chemical in the body? And if so, could it then also be possible that a kind of self-willed positive 'catalyst', a psychological catalyst, could somehow initiate the reversal of the destructive activity of an illness? I know it probably sounds a little wacky, but do you think there could be anything like that, whereby cancer patients could reverse their condition simply by, for example, their mental attitude?"

"You're asking me if it is possible for people to control their own physical well being mentally, just by being absolutely positive and upbeat in their lives?"

"Exactly. That whole positive energy thing, do you think there's anything to it?"

Dr. Richards pondered the question before responding, "Yes, I do believe this sort of thing has been achieved by some people, to some degree. Certainly there have been plenty of recorded cases of people who've demonstrated seemingly magical mental control over their own physiology.

"But while I'm aware that there have been these individual miracles, if we want to call them that, I have yet to be convinced that anyone really understands this sort of thing very well. I know that some people, usually religious people and New Age believers mostly, sometimes claim to, but I don't personally know of anyone in the medical community who can explain how that all works - explain it to the rest of the world's satisfaction, anyway. In a more observable way, though, I think your quitting smoking was the best thing you ever did for your health."

"Okay, so I'm going to live only four to six more months if I'm lucky, according to what those lab tests are telling you. Since this is my reality and I can't do a damned thing to change it, not even by continuing to take the cancer treatment, my question is, how should I spend my last few months on Earth?"

"Well, Daren, keeping it in mind that I'm just a physician and not a spiritual counselor, I'd simply suggest trying to live as healthy as you can, spend your time wisely, and make every one of your days as fruitful as you can. This idea you've mentioned about trying to reverse your situation with a positive outlook certainly can't hurt, can it? You really have nothing at all to lose by channeling only positive energy. But you'll have to believe in it and really practice it, and give it a fair chance. In other words, don't let yourself become discouraged if the results you want aren't immediate. I would just be careful about getting your hopes up too much."

That night Daren went to bed early. He was starting to feel the effects of the beer, something that typically never occurred to him before he had the cancer after consuming anything less than at least a six-pack or more, and it was making him unusually sleepy. He didn't even watch any television at all, which was unusual for him. He felt as though he'd been given a powerful drug to render him unusually drowsy, but all he had had were those three bottles of beer, earlier in the day.

The next morning he woke up with more of a sense of being alive than he had felt in a long time. He was still able to feel some of the effects of the cancer in his body, but he felt well rested for a change. The fact that he was still here, that he hadn't ended it all the day before as he had almost done, was something worth thinking about. For some reason he couldn't explain, he was suddenly very glad that he was still here.

It was the faint but steady clicking sound coming from the hallway that first woke him up. When he climbed out of bed and went to investigate, he discovered that it was the little battery powered alarm clock that he kept in the bathroom. It wasn't loud by any measure, but its second hand clicked with every movement. How odd it was that he'd never noticed that sound before, he thought, even whenever he was in the bathroom, and now he was able to hear it all the way from his bedroom.

He remembered that he needed to pack up everything he owned and move out of the house. He had only two more days in which to get that done, and it looked like he would be doing it all himself. His ex-wife, Amy, wanted no involvement in his life now. His best friend from work, Chad, was working longer hours now since Daren had been laid off, so he wouldn't be available to help him. His cousin, Mike, had a full-sized pickup truck he often loaned to Daren whenever he needed to move big things, but he recently moved to another state over a thousand miles away. His next-door neighbor and occasional drinking buddy, Phil, was presently not speaking to him after

Daren had shot Phil's parakeet with his air rifle three months earlier, after they'd both been drinking a lot of beer. And he couldn't think of anyone else to call at the moment for help.

"I deserve this predicament for the way I've been treating people," Daren heard himself declare aloud to his own surprise. It was not his usual habit lately to accept responsibility for his own troubles. Instead he had become accustomed to always looking for someone else to blame for just about everything. Now, suddenly, he was viewing things very differently. It was almost as if he had been given some kind of special vision. He could see things from outside of his own limited perspective somehow, like he was someone else. And things appeared much more clearly. But that didn't really make any sense at all to him.

Suddenly he remembered how much Phil always enjoyed riding his dirt bike but never seemed to have it in his own budget to buy himself one. It was a crazy idea Daren told himself, but he immediately walked the motorcycle over to the driveway next-door, lowered the kickstand and parked it along the edge where it wouldn't be in the way of a car backing out of the garage, and then he rang the doorbell. It was still early enough in the morning that Phil wouldn't have left for work yet.

When Phil answered the door he didn't say anything, but he gave Daren a dirty look. Daren was grateful that Phil hadn't slammed the door on him.

"Phil, I'm incredibly sorry about what I did to your bird, I really, really am. It was a dirty rotten thing to do, and I've been thinking a lot about it lately. As a token of my sincerity, I want to give you my Honda CRF450. Here, it's yours. I know you've been wanting a bike like this for a while," he handed Phil the keys, and pointed behind him to the bike on the edge of Phil's driveway. Phil accepted the keys reluctantly, and he was speechless.

"It's got a full tank of gas," Daren added, "and I will go right now and sign the title over to you."

So that was one less thing he would have to worry about dealing with now. He suddenly felt relieved about what to do with that bike, and he felt it would be in good hands. Now he had to think about some of his furniture and other bulky possessions. His nice coffee table, table lamp, chairs, kitchen table, bed, bookcase, books, TV and stereo would all need a good home as well. Some of those things were expensive when he bought them, and all were still in excellent condition. But he wasn't going to need any of them now, and he would have no place to store them, anyway.

Before the day was done he had given away all of his largest worldly possessions to the local Goodwill. After he called them they sent two burly young men and a flatbed truck to his house to load up everything he wanted them to take, which included pretty much everything he owned other than his car, his clothing, his sleeping bag, shaving kit, and a few other small odds and ends he thought he might still need. Also before the day was done he had cleaned up the entire house - scrubbed the toilet and shower, cleaned the windows and bathroom mirror, vacuumed the carpet-covered flooring, mopped the kitchen floor, and mowed the yard before calling Mr. Harrington on the phone to tell him that he would be out of the house a day earlier than he was required to be, and that Mr. Harrington could keep all of the deposit.

The sudden realization hit him like a brick that he was now emotionally accepting his fate, and he felt a kind of eagerness to put his past wrongs right. He wasn't absolutely sure that he could ever actually do that completely, especially within the amount of time he had left, but he was suddenly, strangely committed now to working toward that goal.

He felt his throat thirsting for a taste of ice-cold beer, but he had no more beer, and in the back of his mind he heard himself saying that a drink wouldn't satisfy his thirst, anyway. His mind suddenly seemed stronger than his body, at least at the moment.

Chapter 2

The New Challenge

◊

Now he had no place to live. He had maybe enough money to rent a cheap motel room for two weeks. After that he would be homeless, at least until he found a place to stay. Even so, this seemed like just another minor worldly detail to him now. In four to six months, he realized, finding a place to live would no longer be any concern for him.

Amy, his ex-wife, now lived in an apartment a few miles away. Daren hadn't had any communication with her in over six months, but he guessed she still worked at her same job. Something within him made him want to go talk to her. He knew that speaking to him would be the last thing in the world *she* would want right now, but he nevertheless needed to say some things. There were certain things that needed to be said before it was too late.

Amy worked as a sales clerk at a local department store, and the first time Daren stopped by to see her she wasn't on shift. He didn't want to call her on the phone because he figured that she would just hang up on him. And he didn't want to go by her apartment because he was pretty sure she'd just slam the door in his face. But he felt he needed to talk with her in person.

The second day when he visited the store she was working, and fortunately the store was not very busy when he saw her, giving him the perfect opportunity to approach her. When she finally noticed him she immediately turned away, exactly like he had expected her to do. But he was determined to get her to acknowledge him. He was determined to talk to her.

"Amy, I really need to talk to you. I have something to say and it's important."

She turned around to face him, reluctantly. Her body language expressed her desire for him to say what he came to say as quickly as possible and then go away.

"What do you want to tell me, Daren?" she asked quietly so as to avoid creating a disturbance in the store. "And please make it quick because you know how they are here about employees discussing their own personal matters while on the sales floor."

"I want to tell you how sorry I am that for all those years I was such a jerk. I know I really was, and I want to set right my past wrongs. I believe I'm a different man now, and I was hoping..."

"No way," she interrupted him, now raising her voice

unintentionally. "There's no way that I can just forget all of that misery you put me through for a long, long time because now you're suddenly feeling remorseful. I don't think you can ever set right everything you've done, because you would have to grasp the magnitude of it, and you probably never will be able to. But you're hoping... what? That I'll say, oh, it's okay now, just like it never happened? Was *that* what you were hoping for?"

"Your forgiveness," he said, "was all I was hoping for. I realize I can't undo things that were done, but I came here to ask you for forgiveness. Like I said, I'm a changed man now."

She shook her head as tears began forming in her eyes, "I'm sorry, I can't. You stole that whole part of my life – I gave you the best part of my life, and you crushed it under the heel of you shoe like I was lower than dirt. No, Daren, I can't just forgive and forget all of that. You will have to reap what you've sown. That's all I have to say to you, and if I see you in this store again I will call security to remove you from the property."

With that she turned and walked away, and he noticed that before she disappeared through a doorway posted "employees only" she never turned back around to look at him even once.

If ever a door had been slammed in his face with an exclamation of finality, this would have to be it. He knew she meant what she said, and he knew she was right in so many ways. He had treated her in their marriage exactly as badly as she had just reminded him. He'd been abusive, selfish, dishonest, and irresponsible in every way.

To his surprise he didn't feel insulted or humiliated by

her verbal slap in his face, or harbor any ill feelings towards her at all. He simply knew she was right, and for the first time he actually sympathized with her position. He thought about how he used to react to that kind of slap. He used to get defensive automatically, whether someone else was right or not. It was clear to him that he had noticeably changed as a human being. It might be too late for any kind of change to make a huge difference in his world, but he must have changed. He could see the change in himself as if through someone else's eyes.

He still felt the frustration and despair in making up for his past wrongs. This was beginning to seem like an impossible task now. Maybe it just wasn't meant to happen. Maybe this was his justice being served to him in an unexpected manner. It would seem to make perfect sense to him that way.

He decided to stop in at the bar on his way home. The bar contained some familiar surroundings, and he felt that he needed familiar surroundings at the moment. He often popped in for a few drinks, especially whenever he'd get depressed over anything, which wasn't exactly a rare thing lately. He knew the bartender, Dobbs, pretty well. He'd been visiting the bar almost regularly for a number of years, and Dobbs had been tending the same place for at least as many.

"I'll have a cold one on the counter there for you in just a second, Daren," Dobbs said, noticing him take a seat in his usual spot out of the corner of his eye while he finished mixing a drink for another customer.

"Take your time, Dobbs. I plan to spend a few hours in here this afternoon anyway, since, well, since I don't have my beautiful wife to go home to anymore," he said, almost as if he were making the disappointing observation for the first time. "Not that I was going home to her all that much when I *did* have her, and of course I eventually lost her as you know, entirely of my own doing. But it really hit me today, how I've screwed up."

When the frosted glass and the full beer bottle were placed on the counter in front of him he looked up at Dobbs, "I really don't envy you, Dobbs, having to hear these same old depressing sob stories each and every night."

He poured beer from the bottle into the glass, then watched the top foam rise.

"Oh, hell no, Daren. Oddly enough I'm pretty sure that I'd miss all of this if I left this job. Kind of like the housewife who gets hooked on the daytime soaps. I kind of like following peoples' lives, even the sad ones. You kind of get hooked on the life stories after a while. In my job I get to follow the life stories of the regular customers."

"Have you heard any life stories in this bar that are any different from everyone else's story?" Daren asked with a hint of skepticism.

"Oh yeah, you'd be surprised at how the stories are all unique. Pretty messed up, most of them I would have to say, but all are definitely unique in one aspect or another.

"For example, this one guy who comes in here almost every Friday night around nine o'clock just got divorced from his wife. I'm sure you've seen him before, but you probably don't know him because he hangs with a different bunch of friends. Lloyd Price is a hell of a good pool player – spends a lot of his free time playing over at the Billiard Station.

"Anyway, he's always been a control freak, and I've known him for some time. He was always friendly enough to me and to most of his buddies here, when everything goes his way that is, but he's got a temper, and he was apparently beating his lovely wife, Lisa. She finally divorced him recently and got a restraining order against him. What is particularly sad is that they have an eight year-old son. The son idolizes his dad, but his dad is prohibited by that court order from seeing either of them."

"That's sad, all right," Daren remarked, "but that story doesn't sound really all that unique, unfortunately. I've heard lots of stories just like it all of my life – dysfunctional families, husbands beating their wives, divorced couples with kids..."

"What makes this story unique," the bartender countered, "is that the little boy has cancer, and he isn't expected to live even one more year. His dad is an emotional basket case over the whole thing and he feels helpless to do anything about it. He's been drinking more lately than he ever used to drink before. I notice those little details. But as totally messed up as we might say that he is, the man down deep really loves his son. I've never followed any other story exactly like that one, and as you know I've been bartending for quite a while. It's about as sad a story as they get."

"It is sad, all right, but maybe that man is simply reaping what he has sown," Daren said, hearing himself using Amy's words that she spoke to him not more than a half hour before.

By the time Daren left the bar he was already too

drunk to see straight. He made a promise to Dobbs that he wouldn't be driving his car home. The reality was that he no longer had a home to go home to now since he had not yet reserved a motel room, although he hadn't shared that much of his own story with Dobbs. He was planning to simply sleep in his car for a few days until he figured out something better. He left his car in the parking lot of the bar on Dobbs' suggestion.

Across town was a nice little park with a small lake where the ducks could be as much of an attraction as a nuisance. It was only a mile and a half walk. He thought the trip might help him sober up some. He had a wool military blanket in his car, and he had folded it and rolled it up tight before stuffing it into his little backpack. He remembered those long wooden benches in the park, under those huge shady trees, and that the place was usually pretty quiet after the sun went down. He thought it would be a decent place to stretch out for the evening. It was a nice little park, not known for harboring the kind of drug addicts, muggers, or any of the gang activity one might encounter in some of the parks in bigger cities. He expected to be relatively safe there through the night.

Somehow he found his way through town on foot all the way to the park, even as blurry-eyed inebriated as he was. He found the benches just as he remembered them, and they were empty. With a woolen stocking cap covering his head he rolled up in his blanket and stretched out on one of the long benches, his little backpack serving as his pillow. He seemed to be alone in the park now as the sun dipped below the landscape. Eventually the park security might come around and force him to leave he expected, but in the meantime he would relax and try to sleep off some of his intoxication.

The last thing he remembered thinking before drifting off into unconsciousness was that he had completely failed in his initial effort to surrender his old ways. How much had he *really* changed, anyway? Suddenly he was having doubts about this whole change of disposition path he'd set himself on. He wasn't too sure whether or not he had changed at all, or whether he ever actually could.

He was awakened out of a deep sleep by the sense of being thumped on his blanket by what felt like a stiff broomstick. His eyes popped open to the light of dawn, and he perceived the silhouette of a person sitting on his same bench, just past his feet. Forcing his eyes a little wider he finally recognized the form. It was that old bearded white haired man, Tom, and he had apparently swatted the top of Daren's blanket with that hardwood cane of his.

"You again?" Daren asked with surprise. "Where'd you come from?"

"Oh, I've actually been sitting here for quite a while, my friend. And it is time for you to get up. I didn't save you from yourself only to see you find another method of self destruction to follow."

Daren sat up and rubbed his bloodshot eyes. "Again I feel compelled to ask you old man...Tom, I mean. How is my personal life any of your concern?"

"Everything about your life is my *main* concern right now," Tom said.

Daren suddenly began to feel nauseated and hoped he could resist the urge to vomit. He believed he could hold it down for now, but he knew already that this was going to be a very long and unpleasant day.

"Who are you exactly? Or maybe I should be asking *what* are you? Are you like an angel, or some kind of spirit maybe? You don't really look to me like a wizard or a witch. I'd almost expect to see you wearing a robe, if that was it. You *could* be some kind of psychic I suppose, but what about a prophet? That would make the most sense to me. But it's pretty weird how you just appear, as if out of thin air, and then you seem to know everything. Normal people don't do that. I almost feel like I'm in that old movie, *It's A Wonderful Life*. Maybe we should be listening for the sound of a bell, signaling when you'll get your wings," Daren joked in spite of the discomfort of his hangover.

Tom didn't seem at all amused. His demeanor was very serious and matter of fact.

"As I previously indicated, Daren, I'm a catalyst in your life. If you see me as a prophet I won't deny it. My only purpose is to help you change into a better person. I know things about your life that no one else would likely know. I'm not the only one with this particular gift, you know."

"I didn't know there were others like you. But a gift, huh? Seems like that would be more of a curse than a gift."

"This gift allows us to help people. There is nothing cursed about being given that ability, unless we were to neglect helping those who needed our help, of course."

"And you're here to help me, right?"

"I am, and I will. You, Daren, are in serious need of my help. You will in turn help others. That man who visits the bar every Friday night. The bartender told you about him. You can help that man and his family."

"But how could I do that? I have my own problems to keep me busy. I can't even mend my past offenses against my ex-wife."

"Amy will be a challenge for you, all right, but you mustn't give up on her. She loved you deeply, enough to endure years of your abuses. But she has to see with her own eyes the kind of person you really are changing into – the person you will be from now forward. You'll have to find a way to show her that. It will take some time to undo what you spent years doing. But you absolutely must not go back to drinking like you did last night. That probably took a few months off of your life, and you simply don't have extra months to spare."

"That man the bartender told me about – he beats his wife! What am I supposed to do to fix that? I don't have any way to prevent a man from beating his wife. And even if I could help him, why would I want to help some jerk who beats his wife?"

"You were also beating your wife, Daren. Maybe not necessarily with your fist, but psychologically and verbally, you beat her up regularly in the last years of your marriage. She lives with the emotional scars you left her with. That man you are going to help has his anger issues, but he is a lot like you in the sense that he genuinely wants to change. When his son was diagnosed with cancer, it completely and permanently changed that man. Now he needs your help."

"I'm feeling sick to my stomach and my head feels like it will explode. Can't we talk about all of this stuff tomorrow rather than right now?" Daren said.

"We will definitely talk again tomorrow. There is a drinking fountain over there," Tom pointed toward the park's drinking fountain, "and I would suggest that you drink as much water as you possibly can."

Daren didn't even watch Tom walk away. He closed his eyes and took a deep breath before forcing himself up onto his feet. When he did open his eyes to view his surroundings, Tom was already gone. He did as Tom recommended and drank as much water as he could get down. It seemed to help right away, at least some.

Before the day was done Daren had walked all the way back to his car parked outside the bar where Dobbs worked, after having puked several times in the gutters along the way, and he then drove to the nearest motel. He rented a room for ten days.

When his head hit the pillow as he stretched out horizontally on the clean bed, he was able to rest finally, and really relax. He was starting to feel a little better now. Before falling asleep he did a lot of thinking about a lot of different things. His future, whatever was left of it, looked especially uncertain to him now. He had absolutely no idea about what he needed to do when tomorrow arrived. He decided not to try too hard to figure it all out right now.

Chapter 3

Unforeseen Turns

◊

The doorbell caught Amy by surprise, because she had just finished talking with her friend, Sally, over the phone less than ten minutes earlier. Sally lived about three miles away, and she told Amy that she would be right over. The two of them planned to meet up with some of their other friends and they were all going out to an upscale nightclub later on for socializing and dancing, and hopefully meeting single men. She was thinking about how amazing it was that Sally could be at the door already. When she heard the doorbell she was still in the bathroom putting on her makeup.

When she opened the door she was not only surprised, but also visibly annoyed to see Daren standing there. He was clean-shaven and wearing fine clothing, with a small cap on his head to help hide the fact that he had lost most of his hair. In his left hand was a single yellow rose, which he extended to her. She refused to take it.

"What are you doing here, Daren? Wasn't I clear enough the other day when I said I don't want to see you again? I don't want to talk to you. I don't want to know anything about you. What do I have to do to make you understand that?"

"I understand it, Amy. I was just hoping that we could be friends again, like we used to be back before we got married. I'm a changed man now with a new disposition. A lot has happened in my life recently, and I've really changed a lot. May I come in? I really want to talk to you."

"No, Daren. We have nothing to talk about anymore. Even if I could find it in me to forgive you for what you've done to me, I'm not so sure I could ever forget everything. There is nothing that you could say or do now to fix all of what you have done, so you might as well stop trying. You've had thousands of chances to do that. Don't even waste your time trying now. By the way, what happened to your hair? That little hat doesn't hide it very well, and you weren't even wearing it the other day. Not that I care or anything, but..."

"Cancer treatments. I finally stopped taking them. I got the diagnosis a few months ago. The cancer was detected a bit too late to do very much about it. I took those treatments for a while, but... Long story, but none of it really matters anymore. I'm going to spend the rest of my days helping other people, and making up for the things I've messed up in my life. I know I have a lot of work to do, but I feel blessed that I have been given this opportunity. That's what I have to do. I mean it's what I *want* to do."

She laughed, "Nice try, Daren, but it won't work. I've fallen for your sympathy tricks too many times in the past. I suppose next you were going to tell me that your doctor gave you only six more months to live. Isn't that pretty much how the story is supposed to go? You had your head shaved just to make it believable. Your deceptions have become much too predictable by now, Daren."

"Actually, it's *four* to six months, and that's if I'm lucky he said. But I didn't make all this up, and I'm not here for your sympathy. The cancer specialist, Dr. Richards, goes to the same church you go to. He's told me that he knows you. You can ask him yourself if you don't believe me about the cancer."

"You're not my husband anymore, so really it's none of my business, anyway."

"I know that I really blew what I had with you, Amy, but I never for one minute stopped being in love with you, even though I completely failed repeatedly when it came to showing it. I realize that the best I can hope for now is that we can someday be friends again."

She shook her head, "I don't think we can ever again be friends. The man I married no longer exists. That man wasn't selfish, devious, or insensitive. I thought he was my friend, but he changed into somebody else – somebody I don't like very much a long time ago."

"It's true that I'm no longer the same in every way as that person you exchanged wedding vows with, but I'm a lot closer to him than the man you divorced."

He could see the tears forming in her eyes, and she seemed to be anxious to close the door and end their conversation.

"Look, Daren, I'm sorry about your illness, if it's real. Your life has been a tragedy, and it saddens me more than you will ever know. But you and I are done. It's over between us. Can you understand that? I have worked hard to get my life back since the divorce, and I'm finally able to move on. Now you need to, too."

After she said it she closed the door. She anxiously hoped he would be gone by the time Sally arrived. She was aware that this encounter had affected her whole mood, and she hoped she could forget all about it by the time she met with her friends. But she wasn't going to be able to forget any of it for the rest of the evening, no matter how hard she tried.

Daren turned his attention to the man he was requested to help. He felt clueless about how he might possibly help that man, because Tom gave him no specific ideas about how to do it. He could go ask Dobbs for more information about him, but of course that would mean another visit to the bar and more drinking. He could wait until he saw Tom again – he remembered that Tom assured him they would be talking again tomorrow. Well, today was tomorrow already. Where was that little prophet anyway, now that he needed to talk to him?

Daren decided to spend an hour or two in the local public library that afternoon, searching for motivational self-help material. He was in there, reaching for a book that was sitting on a high shelf when he heard Tom's voice behind him.

"Excellent choice, that book," Tom said, "I must have read it myself at least four times over the last six or seven years. It is considered one of the best on the subject of turning over a new leaf in life."

Daren turned around with the book in his hand.

"Why am I not surprised to see you in here?" he said.

"Lloyd Price," the old man said.

"What?"

"The man you will help – remember? The bartender told you his name is Lloyd Price? His ex-wife is Lisa Price."

Daren thought the names sounded familiar, but he had forgotten that Dobbs had mentioned their names when he was telling Daren their story.

"Okay, now that I am reminded of their names, just exactly how am I supposed to help them? What am I supposed to do for them? Surely you have some ideas in mind about that."

"You are more creative and resourceful than the average guy, Daren. You've always been perfectly able to apply your creativity toward manipulating people to get your own way with things. Now you just have to apply your creative genius towards a different purpose. What I *will* tell you is where you can find Lloyd. He'll be playing pool Monday night after he gets off work, but not in the bar you normally go to. Have you ever been to the Billiard Station?"

"Yes. It's been a few years, but I've been in there."

"Well, he gets off work at eight o'clock on Monday nights and he's usually at that place before nine, so you should be able to find him there the evening after tomorrow around about that time."

"What does he look like, and what about his ex-wife, Lisa? Where might I find her?"

"One step at a time, Daren. Besides, I have to leave *some* of the work for you to do here. After all, you're the one with the creativity when it comes to figuring these kinds of things out. I'm just the catalyst. If you are going to really change your life you are going to have to put forth some effort.

"By the way, I did forget to mention that you should soon notice, if you haven't already, your senses becoming more acutely tuned now than they ever were before. You'll have clearer perception and better intuition about most things, but you'll feel things more, including any kind of pain. You'll notice having more sensitivity to everything around you and within you, but it just means you're more alive now. It's all part of your transformation. But you should learn to trust your senses from now on, because they won't let you down."

Daren went directly from the library home to his motel room and started reading the book he'd checked out, and he didn't stop reading it until he had read the whole thing, cover to cover. He didn't even take any breaks from it for lunch or for dinner. By the time he had finished reading the book the sun had gone down, and he was exhausted. He was asleep before eight o'clock, and he slept like a baby all night long. Then the next day, Sunday, he spent almost the whole day re-reading the whole book. He just couldn't seem to get enough of it.

When Monday night arrived, he found himself in the Billiard Station pool hall exactly as Tom had instructed, wondering how he was going to identify this Lloyd Price character both Tom and Dobbs had mentioned.

When the clock on the wall behind the bar showed the time to be nine o'clock, Daren looked over at one pool table and then another until he found the one with the largest gathering of pool players. He decided to focus his attention on those individuals, to see if he remembered any of their faces from the bar he normally visited. He also watched the game in hopes of getting a sense about the skill level of each player. He remembered what Dobbs had said about the man being an excellent pool player.

After watching a few games he thought several of the guys looked familiar, and it was hard to pick out one player more skilled than the others. One of the guys sitting at the closest booth stood out from the others in Daren's mind for some reason, but he couldn't put his finger on why. He finally decided to interrupt their game and simply ask for Lloyd.

"I am looking for a man named Lloyd Price," he said, "would anyone here know him?"

That same man sitting at the booth Daren had the strongest sense about stood up with his cue stick in his hand. He was bigger and taller than Daren, standing maybe an inch above six feet, and he must have weighed forty or fifty more pounds. In Daren's view he had a rough look about him. Daren's first impression of the guy was that he could certainly be intimidating if he chose to be. More often than not Daren's first impressions would tend to be spot-on about the people he met.

"I'm Lloyd Price," the man said, "Who are you and what do you want?"

"My name is Daren McBride. I'd like to ask you a few questions, mainly concerning your ex-wife. I didn't mean to interrupt your pool game, though. Would it be better if I came back at another time? I'd prefer speaking with you privately if at all possible."

"What is your business with my ex-wife?" the man asked with a hint of suspicion.

"My questions aren't only concerning your ex-wife, Mr. Price, but about you, too," Daren said.

He learned quickly and the hard way that something he said was the wrong thing to say to Mr. Lloyd Price, because without any warning the man swung the pool cue across Daren's face and it struck him right above his upper lip. Daren recoiled from it and grabbed his face, yelling, "Ouch! What was that for?"

"I've got nothing to say to any lawyer or investigator working for Lisa. If you know what's good for you, mister, you'll leave before I break one of these sticks over your head and shove the splintered end down your throat. Everyone in here has known me for a long time and they'll make better witnesses for me than they ever will for you."

Daren's nose started bleeding, and he pressed one hand on it to stop the flow.

"I sure wish people would stop hitting me with sticks," he complained. "Look, Lloyd, I don't work for your ex-wife. I don't presently work for anyone, unfortunately. I've never even met your ex-wife, but I'm neither a lawyer nor an investigator. My mission is simply to help you personally manage certain difficulties you are presently facing, as unpleasant as this task now looks like it is going to be. I know all about your son's illness. I have terminal cancer, too. I'm here to help you and your family if you'll let me do that. As crazy as I know it sounds, my information is that you can really use my help right now, and at the same time I also need yours. Please don't ask me how I know anything about you and your ex-wife, or about your son, or why I should want to help you. It is a very unbelievable set of circumstances."

It was suddenly quiet enough in the pool hall that anyone in the room would seem to be able to hear a pin drop. Lloyd was momentarily speechless. He obviously didn't know what to think about what Daren had just said.

One of the players appeared to shift his attention to the cue balls on the table, and he was re-chalking the tip of his stick when he broke the silence, "Is that true, Lloyd, about your little boy being sick?"

"Yeah, it's true," said Lloyd with a sober look on his face, "as much as I wish it weren't. I haven't been talking about it much except for maybe a few times when I've had too much to drink because, well, maybe I've kind of been in denial about it. But I don't know how this guy here knows anything about it, or just what he thinks he can do about it."

One of the other players handed Daren a handkerchief for his nosebleed.

"I can't do anything to cure his cancer," Daren responded, taking the handkerchief and holding it to his nose with one hand, "but I *can* help the boy learn how to live with it, just as I've had to learn how to get along with my own condition. I could have a talk with him, and I could have a talk with your wife... I mean your ex-wife, if that's okay with you. I believe it could help. Maybe I can

35

change her way of thinking about you, and your son's way of thinking about his cancer. Not exactly my business I know, but who cares, right? If peoples' lives can be made better, then that's all that matters, right?"

Lloyd thought about what Daren just said, and he seemed to like what he heard, even as weird as it all sounded. He was not accustomed to people offering their help to him for any reason, and this Daren McBride, even though he was a complete stranger, seemed at least genuine.

"So, let me get this straight," Lloyd said, "you're saying that you would actually help me and my family, even after I've whacked you with my pool stick like I did?"

"Well, my nose and upper lip do hurt – I didn't much enjoy being hit with that stick. But to answer your question, yes, I came here tonight specifically to find a way to help you. That's how I can help my own situation, by helping you with yours. I'm on this mission, and you might say I am being guided by a prophet."

There was some chuckling among the guys, and Daren decided to laugh along with them, to lighten up the atmosphere. Lloyd Price seemed more serious.

"Maybe you can ask that prophet about which numbers you should pick for the lottery," someone remarked in a mocking manner that stirred a few more laughs among Lloyd's buddies. Daren noticed that Lloyd still wasn't laughing.

"I realize that all this talk about a prophet and about me being on this goodwill mission probably makes me come across as some kind of nutcase," Daren said, looking into their faces, first one and then another of each of the guys standing around tuning in with a natural curiosity, "but I'm telling this as I believe it to be. I've never in my life been very religious or superstitious at all, but that prophet knows things that nobody else knows. If not for him I'd have put an end to my own existence days ago. But instead here I am, and I'm compelled now to change peoples' lives for the better."

If any of those present perceived him as a kook, Lloyd Price certainly didn't appear to. Maybe it was more that he *wanted* to believe what Daren was saying than actually being convinced, but either way it didn't matter. Either way Daren was determined to find a way to help him make positive changes in his life.

"My own ex-wife wouldn't even consider talking to me right now if I were to offer her money," Daren said, "so I know first-hand how frustrating things can be with an ex-wife. Your situation is really a lot like mine in some ways, Lloyd, except that I don't have a son. But I do have the cancer, and I can relate to your son about that."

"Did your prophet tell you everything about my ex-wife and me?" Lloyd asked him.

"Everything that he thinks I should know, except where I can find your son and ex-wife. Apparently he wanted me to obtain that information the hard way. Nothing is very easy at all about the things that prophet compels me to do, I've come to learn."

Lloyd asked for a piece of paper and something to write with, and one of his buddies promptly produced both items and handed them to him. He scribbled something on part of the paper, tore it free from the other section and folded it up. Then he wrote an address on the other half and handed both pieces to Daren.

"That is where my ex-wife and son live," he said, "I'm not supposed to have any contact with them, because of a restraining order, but maybe you could give them that message for me. Would you be able to do that, Mr. McBride?"

Daren took the papers and stuck them into his pocket with his free hand, and looked into Lloyd's eyes. He could see the hopeful sincerity in his eyes, and for the first time since he'd met him, he really *wanted* to help him.

"I will," he assured him.

The guys resumed their pool game as if there had been no interruption, and before he forgot, Daren told Lloyd the name of the motel and room number where he was staying, just in case Lloyd wanted to find him and talk some more.

"There is a way to let go of all the anger that builds up inside," Daren told him when the others no longer appeared to be paying any attention. "If you're ever interested I would be happy to show you how you can do that - I know first-hand that it works. I have learned some truly amazing things in recent days – things that have completely changed my life."

This was the first time in a long time that Daren felt as though he was actually making solid progress with any worthwhile endeavor. He was making progress, and he was feeling inspired about it. There was an eagerness within him now to continue his mission that he hadn't felt previously, and it felt good.

When he left the pool hall he stopped by a convenience

store on his way back to his motel room to buy a small bag of ice and a box of zip-seal bags with which to create an icepack for his swollen lip. The pain was throbbing, but his tolerance for physical pain now seemed much higher than he ever remembered it being. He reminded himself that his throbbing lip was really the least of his concerns right now.

When he approached the front door of the old singlewide mobile home the following morning, where Lisa Price and her son now resided according to Lloyd, Daren suddenly felt a strange sadness inside him that he couldn't understand at first. It wasn't until she answered the door and he saw the scars on her face that he realized where the feeling came from. Her face bore the evidence of physical abuse, and even though the skin of her facial wounds had completely healed, the emotional damage still showed in her eyes. Those kinds of wounds were going to take longer to heal.

"Lisa Price?"

"Yes?"

"Hi Lisa, my name is Daren McBride, and I would like to talk to you about your ex-husband, Lloyd Price, and also about your son."

"Are you Lloyd's attorney, or one of his buddies?"

"No ma'am. I'm not an attorney, and I just met Lloyd for the first time yesterday," he said, and then laughed. "I got a fat lip from our meeting."

"What is your business with Lloyd then, Mr. McBride, and what do you want to know about my son?"

"I know about your son's illness," he said, removing his hat to reveal his own hair loss, "and I think I can help him because I also have cancer. May I have a talk with him?"

"He's not here right now," she said, as the tears started rolling down her cheeks. "I had to take him into the hospital last night. That…damned leukemia started getting bad again. It's just horrible. That's where he is now - they want to keep him there and closely monitor his condition for a few days."

"Well, I can come back later. But please try not to worry yourself too much, Mrs. Price. I know that it seems impossible to keep from worrying about those we love, but things have a way of turning out better than we expect when we fear the worst. I've always been the biggest worrywart about every little thing, but I'm learning now about letting go of anguish, anxiety, fear, resentment, paranoia - all of the negative emotions, and how to see the better side of things. We can't always see it, but there is always a better side."

"Are you like a preacher?"

"No, I'm not. I don't consider myself a religious man, or at least I never did before. But my perspective about things, about life sure has changed a lot lately."

He suddenly reached into his pants pocket and pulled out the folded paper that Lloyd had given him to give to Lisa. He handed it to her.

"I almost forgot," he said, "but Lloyd asked me to give you this. I don't know what he wrote, but it seemed pretty important to him that I give it to you."

"Would you like to come inside?" she asked him after he handed her the paper, "I can brew a pot of coffee if you'd like some."

"Yes, I would very much love a hot cup of coffee right now, Mrs. Price. And if you have the time I do have quite a story to tell you – it's an amazing story really. Whether or not you choose to believe any of it is up to you of course, but I'm pretty sure you'll find it inspiring."

"I have plenty of time today," she said, "especially for an inspirational kind of story."

Chapter 4

Requesting a Miracle

◊

Daren's body had taken a hard beating from the cancer before it went into remission, and even when he tried to forget the worst of the physical symptoms, the illness shouted in his face. It was his obsession with staying on course with his mission that got him up and going.

He reflected on the conversation they'd had the day before, he and Lisa Price. He had told her his own story, including how shamefully he had treated his ex-wife for a long time until she finally left him. He described the person he had become as basically rotten to the core, until something suddenly changed his life drastically. He explained to Lisa that there had been a turning point in his life that made him want to change.

"It's like that with your ex-husband, Mrs. Price. I saw it in his eyes. He is in that transformation phase where he is beginning to see the mistakes he's made, and he hates those mistakes he's made. He's going to be obsessed with making things right again, no matter how hard that will be."

"How can you be so sure of that?" she asked him. "Lloyd can be just unbelievably violent and mean. See these scars on my face? He can't control his temper."

"He'll have to work on controlling his temper, that's for sure," Daren had explained, "but your son's illness has completely changed the life of Lloyd Price. He loves his son more than his own life and, even though he's hurt you, Mrs. Price, you are nevertheless much more important to him than he is capable of showing at this point in time."

"You got all of that just from looking into his eyes?" she asked skeptically.

"Well, it's a little more complicated than that, but I am confident that Lloyd is salvageable. I believe I can talk him into attending anger management classes if you'd be willing to allow him at least limited access to his son. I can read that man like a book because part of me is exactly like him. He's emotionally sick as a result of whatever negative forces pushed him around in his distant past, but he really wants to get better. I believe that he can, because he *wants* to change. You can help him change, Mrs. Price."

She seemed quite skeptical of the prospect. She had taken too many of her ex-husband's punches to be able to trust him now. But in spite of everything, thinking about the possibility of being able to actually help Lloyd conquer his inner demons fanned the small candle flame of hope in her mind, and she reminded herself that she had married him years ago because she genuinely cared about him as much as she did. But this also went against common sense. If the man beat her for years without repentance, why should he be given any benefit of the doubt now?

"I would have to agree that you are perfectly justified to think that way, Mrs. Price, given his track record. It would be tragic indeed if my gut sense about your husband turned out to be wrong after you had allowed him back into your life based on my suggestion that he had changed. I'm only seeing things from my own viewpoint, which I realize is biased. But there is perhaps something else to consider here as well. Your son's relationship with his dad – would it not also be tragic if the boy never got to see his father again?"

The words had come out of his mouth before he had given them enough thought, and for a moment he wished he hadn't spoken them. The small living room in her mobile home became very quiet, and he could sense the magnitude of the grief she was feeling.

At first his words reminded him of the kind of insensitive things he had become so used to saying, and he was mad at himself for having said them. But then the more he thought about the matter of her son's relationship with his dad, the more he realized it was an important matter to consider. Daren quickly realized that he had been sent there to talk with her for a very important reason, and that his word choices weren't necessarily all his own.

She started crying uncontrollably, and he handed her the box of facial tissues that he found on a little end table near the sofa. She wiped her eyes and gradually regained her composure.

"My son's name is Austin – he's just eight years old. He worships Lloyd. I didn't want him to grow up to be like Lloyd, but the doctors say he may not even survive another year. He may not have a chance to grow up to be like his dad or anybody else."

"You mentioned that his cancer is leukemia."

"Yes. It's an acute form of leukemia known as ALL, or Acute Lymphoblastic Leukemia. There is a relatively new treatment being done with this form at a hospital in Seattle, the latest variation of a stem cell transplant, that has apparently been about ninety-eight percent successful so far in actually completely curing patients – my understanding is that it's more like a 'procedure' than a typical cancer treatment, but it costs $70,000! We learned that there was no insurance coverage for that under his dad's workplace family health insurance plan, and we haven't been able to raise that kind of money. The crazy thing is that the insurance *will* pay for treatments such as chemotherapy, steroids, and radiation therapy, none of which are expected to save his life, but it won't pay for this procedure that actually would most likely save his life. What's crazy is that ultimately those approved treatments could end up costing the insurance company that much or even more! Neither Lloyd nor I really own any property to speak of that we could sell or borrow against to raise that much money."

"My cancer is a completely different type – it started in

my lungs and spread from there," Daren had told her, "but it's also terminal, and I understand the frustration. Mine has no reliable cure in my advanced stage, and according to my doctor I will be gone inside of six months. If I could mend my past wrongs with my ex-wife before it's too late, I would be more at peace with my own fate, and I know that's where Lloyd is at right now, too. As for raising the money for Austin's procedure, I would simply urge you to keep all of your hopes alive. Please don't give up on your son by letting go of your hope. I have become a believer in miracles lately, and that's the only thing that has kept me going."

His visit with her had been brief, but he left with a feeling of accomplishment – that he had said exactly what he had been sent there to say. And at least she seemed somewhat open to the possibility of obtaining permission for Lloyd to see his son, and that alone made his visit worthwhile.

Now, the following day, Daren was compelled to force himself out of bed by his desire to find some way to raise seventy thousand dollars to save an eight year-old boy whom he had never met, and to keep working toward repairing the damages of broken relationships. Suddenly his mission had become much more important to him than it was before talking with Lisa Price.

The words of the prophet were now ringing in his ears – everything that Tom had said about his creative resourcefulness, and the higher purpose to which his creativity must be applied - he couldn't get any of those words out of his head. This was a powerful challenge he had ahead of him. Somehow, some way, he would have to raise the money.

He had spent almost an hour trying to come up with some kind of seemingly practical idea about raising a large sum of money when a thought finally hit him, and it stuck in his mind. He knew that some of the larger corporations in society relied heavily on a public image for their success. Effective marketing factors in human emotions. If consumers have a positive "feeling" about one particular name brand or another, they are more likely to buy the products or do business with that brand.

It seemed like a dandy idea, at least in principle, but he struggled to come up with a plan for pursuing it. The goal would be to convince the CEO of a large firm that its profits could be directly enhanced by such an act of generosity. A tough sell perhaps, but that was the pitch Daren felt compelled to make. He just needed to figure out where to make it, and to whom he should make his appeal.

There was that nagging feeling he couldn't seem to completely ignore no matter how hard he tried. He was feeling physically sick again, sicker than he'd been feeling over the past couple of weeks. A warm shower didn't make the feeling go away. But he nevertheless dressed himself in his most professional looking clothes including a sport coat and tie, after he had shaved his face. He also poured eye drops into his eyes in hopes of clearing up some of the bloodshot redness. He wanted to present the best possible image for the professional people he intended to meet on this day. He seemed to start actually feeling a bit better almost as soon as he saw himself in the mirror looking better.

"Daren McBride is it? Hmm, I don't see your name on Mr. Vanderpool's appointment list for today," said the girl at the front desk. "Is he expecting to see you?"

"No, he wouldn't be. But what I have to tell him could improve the public's opinion of this company dramatically. I only want five minutes of his time."

Two minutes later Daren was invited to take a seat in Mr. Vanderpool's office – he was the president and CEO of a nationally marketed dairy products producer, and Daren wasted no time starting into his well-rehearsed sales pitch.

"Can you just imagine, Sir, how people would always be thinking of the little boy who was cured of his deadly cancer every time they were to see your products and your brand name advertised? Your competition wouldn't stand a chance against that kind of goodwill image you would have created by doing that."

After thinking about Daren's proposal for no more than a minute, Mr. Vanderpool politely explained the company's policy on such matters, "We've had to cut back on some of our advertising costs and charitable donations for this year unfortunately to meet our firm's budgetary requirements, and what you have proposed falls into that category of our operating costs. It's certainly a noble cause and I very much appreciate your concern for the boy's welfare - I applaud your effort. But if we were to do that for one little boy we would be expected to do the same and more for other children with similar needs. Once you open up the doors with that kind of commitment there is almost no way to ever close them, and my responsibility as the head of this corporation is to take care of our shareholders, and the financial condition of the company.

Our board members and shareholders watch our balance sheets closely. I am terribly sorry, Mr. McBride, but I will have to decline your offer."

It wasn't like he had expected a different outcome. He knew it was going to be a tough sell, and that was certainly proving to be the case thus far. But his plan had now been rejected by the largest business entity headquartered within a fifty mile radius that he knew of, and he was mindful that if a corporation with its resources couldn't help him, finding another having fewer resources but still willing to do it was going to be quite a challenge indeed.

Right now he really wanted a cigarette. He hadn't smoked even once since his doctor first told him he had cancer, but now suddenly the urge for just one lousy cigarette was a strong one. He had thrown his last pack away more than a month ago, so he didn't have quick and convenient access to any cigarettes at the moment. He contemplated a quick trip to the convenience store only three blocks away for a pack, but for some reason he didn't rush out from his motel room just yet.

He was starting to get the unpleasant feeling that he had failed in his most important mission, and that he was actually starting to regress when he heard the knocking on his motel room door. He knew it had to be either Lloyd or Lisa Price, because they were the only two he had told where he was staying. When he opened the door he was surprised, although he suddenly realized that he shouldn't have really been surprised.

"Tom, how'd you know where I was?" Daren shook his head as if to retract a silly question, "Oh, never mind that. But where is it that *you* live, anyway? I mean, where do you come from when you always just show up? You know you look like a hobo wandering the streets. Don't you have a house to live in? And while we're on this subject, what is your last name? I never did get your full name, or even how I might be able to reach you if I wanted to call or write. The only thing I know about you is that your name is Tom, if indeed it really *is* Tom. That's kind of weird, isn't it, that you haven't told me more about yourself?"

"I'm not here to talk about me, Daren. I'm here because you need my help. Now let's talk about that creative plan of yours for raising money to save that boy, Austin. I know that you've been guilty of a lot of things, but giving up on something important to you has never been one of them. You've always been very good at finding ways around the obstacles you've encountered while trying to get whatever it was you've ever wanted. Take your smoking habit, for example. When your doctor finally convinced you that your smoking was contributing to your health problems, you miraculously found the resolve to stop smoking. You've never been easily pushed off course before, why start now?"

Tom suddenly looked down and remembered the advertising brochure in his hand, and he handed it to Daren, "Oh, I almost forgot. This was hanging here on your doorknob."

Daren took the brochure from Tom and glanced down at it. The elaborate graphics on the front of the glossy stiff paper caught his attention, and he held it up for a closer look. It was a flyer advertising some of the products of a giant clothing manufacturer with the brand name, Mammoth Mens' & Womens' Apparel.

"Man, I'll bet they spent a fortune on this marketing gimmick. Design layout, photography, publication, mass printing, and then distribution – hiring people to go door to door with them. And they'd have to print up tens of thousands of expensive copies to generate any significant sales returns. How much do you figure all of this cost them?"

When he didn't hear any comment from Tom he looked up, but Tom was no longer standing there. Daren looked outside his door to the left and then the right, but there was no sign of Tom anywhere. It was as if the little old man had vanished into thin air, kind of the way it always seemed to be with him. The strangest part about it was that Tom walked with the help of a cane. In Daren's mind there could be simply no way for the old man to be able to move extremely fast.

Daren's attention was immediately drawn back to that brochure in his hand, and he tried hard to think of where he'd seen that company's advertising before. And then finally he remembered where – on a television commercial. He thought about that commercial, and almost immediately he also remembered seeing their ad on a billboard a few months ago while driving on the freeway. Apparently the people running that company believed strongly in advertising, and were willing to spend big to build the name recognition in his community. TV commercials weren't cheap. These fancy brochures weren't cheap. That billboard sign couldn't have been cheap. The wheels in Daren's head were starting to turn.

The people he needed to talk to would be the people who worked in the company's marketing department. He would need to research various advertising costs and then present to that marketing team a profound cost comparison. If it turned out that they were spending considerably more than $70,000 on an advertising campaign that he could convince them was actually less effective than would be the automatic publicity they could expect by saving an eight year-old boy's life, then he'd have them. It was simply a matter of economics, and simple logic.

Once again he felt energized by the thought of it, and his physical pain seemed to completely disappear for the moment. This new plan was a good one and he felt pretty confident about it. He would go to the library and log onto one of their computers. He would research advertising costs. He would write down contact names and phone numbers and purchase a calling card, then go to a public phone because he no longer had a phone, and start making phone calls. He would take lots of notes. And then he would go make an appointment with Mammoth's marketing team, and he'd sell them on his idea. He believed in his idea now, and he was determined this time to make it happen.

Chapter 5

A Door Finally Opens

◊

His presentation was short but convincing. He came prepared with all of the information he needed, and he had even created some useful flip charts to help him illustrate his key points. By the time he had finished saying everything he had come to say, no one in the room could even imagine any reasonable argument that could possibly be made against his proposal. The entire marketing team was sold on this idea, and he could see it in their eyes.

"I realize that these kinds of decisions typically must be approved by top management or maybe voted on in your next board meeting, and that might take some time," Daren said, "but I would just remind everyone that in this

53

unique situation time is especially critical. If Austin doesn't receive this treatment very soon it will be too late for him. His life is literally on the line here."

"Fortunately," explained one of the team members, Lane Darnell, who also happened to be the executive director of marketing, "you won't have to wait for an answer on it. Our department is given quite a bit of discretionary flexibility with these kinds of marketing programs, and we have the budget for it. Mammoth has given us all the authority we need to make it happen, and I for one am totally for doing this. It's a brilliant idea in my opinion, and it's something we can all feel good about doing."

The others in the room each offered their own personal endorsement of the plan, and Daren left the meeting with an exhilarating sense of accomplishment.

He spent the next couple of days trying to think up some creative way to communicate with Amy. Her firmly expressed desire not to talk with him created a challenge unlike any he had ever met before. But Daren remembered what Tom had said, that he shouldn't give up on her. He decided to hand-sketch a cute card that would hopefully appeal to her emotional side, and send it to her in the mail.

Later on in the evening when he heard the knocking on his motel room door, this time his more sensitive hearing told him that it wasn't the prophet. The rhythm, unique sound, and volume of the knocks were different. Daren realized that he would have totally missed noticing those kinds of details even a week earlier, before he had started to change in the ways that he recently had.

"Lloyd Price! Hello my friend, I am really glad you

dropped by – I have been hoping that you would eventually. Please come in and have a seat. I'd offer you a cold beer but I just haven't been to the store yet since getting this room. This is only going to be a very temporary residence for me you know."

Lloyd entered, looked around, and then sat in one of only two chairs in the room, only six feet from the foot of the bed that occupied about a third of the room.

"No problem," he said. "I'm not really here for a drink, anyway. Mainly I just came by to say I was sorry about hitting you with that pool stick the other night, and also to say thank you for what you did for Austin. I was running into one dead end after another trying to come up that kind of money. It's pretty tough to do on my income for sure. And then you made this miracle happen."

"I was very glad to have a part in it. I'm just glad that Austin's got a way to receive that procedure that he needs."

"My boy owes his life to you, Daren McBride, and I …"

Daren interrupted him, "No, Lloyd, as much as I would love to take all of the credit for having saved your son, I was actually not the catalyst that set everything in motion."

"Wait, let me guess – it was your 'prophet' who was behind everything, right?"

Daren nodded, "Yes, that is in fact one-hundred percent true. I merely followed his directions."

"When will I ever get to see this man you see as a prophet? I sure am curious, and I have some things I'd like to say to him, to express my gratitude and everything."

"I can't tell you whether you'll ever meet him or not. It isn't exactly up to me. He just kind of appears whenever he decides to and then disappears about as quickly, when I'm not even looking. I know it all sounds pretty odd. I know."

"Well, odd or not, the only thing I know for sure is that I am grateful for what's been done for my son, and for whatever you did to get my ex-wife to even consider giving me a chance to correct my past wrongs. I *know* you had something to do with that, right, with Lisa agreeing to get the restraining order dropped, at least conditionally anyway?"

"That's great! So, what sort of conditions did Lisa insist on?"

"I have to get help with learning how to control my temper. But I totally agree that it's for the better, and it's something I should have done a long, long time ago. But I am positive now that I will never lay an angry hand on her again, because I am going to learn how to exercise that kind of control over the anger, and as I assume you already know, I really *want* to change into a better man. I'll do whatever it takes this time to keep my old mistakes from ever coming back. But I can't express it in words, the way I feel about being given this second chance, even though I know I don't deserve a second chance."

"Maybe none of us *deserve* a second chance, Lloyd, but I wish it were that we could all have a second chance. I really hope you can make things work out between you and your ex-wife this time around, and make a positive new start with everything."

"Did you know that they're paying for the travel

expenses to Seattle, and even for hotel accommodations in addition to that medical procedure? And not just for Austin, but for Lisa and me, too, so that we can go as a family and be with him for the whole thing. My boss has agreed to give me the time off work for that.

"That's quite a thing for them to do, isn't it? Mammoth Apparel – who would have ever dreamed that a clothing company like that would be willing to pay for such an expensive life-saving procedure, for a little boy they didn't even know? I can't get over it," he cut his rambling short before he choked up completely on his words.

Daren was thinking about how good it felt to see all of this happen. There was nothing about any of it that he could have imagined even a few weeks before. He had to admit to himself that miracles, actual miracles, really *do* happen, and they become visible whenever people open their minds to them. He realized that he wouldn't have been able to admit that before. This was a new perspective for him.

Daren hadn't been coughing up much blood now for over two weeks, and his headaches had been fewer and noticeably less extreme. When it crossed his mind he started getting cautiously optimistic about the cancer. The thought that he might actually be getting well again, that the cancer in his body might be disappearing, was either teasing him in a cruel way, or it was for real. He didn't want to see Dr. Richards just yet, in case it was all just imagined. He wasn't ready to have his bubble popped, so to speak, just yet. Besides, he always dreaded those doctor visits – he dreaded just about everything about them.

It suddenly occurred to him that he hadn't seen Tom in

a while. It had been almost a week since the little old man had knocked on the door of his motel room. Maybe that was a good thing. Maybe it meant that he had been following the right path since that day and no longer needed the prophet to show him the way. Whatever it meant, if anything at all, he began to feel as though he missed that interaction with a person like Tom who seemed to know just about everything. The prophet didn't always answer all of his questions, but whenever he did have an answer for him, the information always turned out to be completely true.

Daren now believed that he had fulfilled his primary obligation laid upon him by the prophet. There had been nothing easy or simple about it, but it was done and behind him. Now he wasn't feeling compelled to tackle any new goals.

Making amends with Amy had seemed to run into a solid wall. He felt clueless about where to go now on that front, if there really was anything else he could possibly do to change her mind about him. He had mailed that card he'd made for her the day before, but what good could that possibly do he started to wonder? Someone doesn't change someone's closed mind simply by reading a homemade card. There was no going back to try talking with her again after all of the ways she expressed her wishes against communicating with him. The door to Amy's heart seemed to be as closed and locked as any door ever could be.

Tom's words, he remembered, were encouraging, telling him not to give up on Amy. He had kept every hope he had about her alive because he wanted to believe in that. But when it came to figuring out some way to change her mind, he had now simply run out of ideas.

He sure wished that he could talk to Tom right now. If only he knew the old man's address he would go pay him a visit right now. But he had never gotten that much out of him. He couldn't stop wondering if Tom even had a regular residence, or if he really was just an old homeless guy out wandering the streets looking for messed up lives to "fix". If the latter were true, then it was amazing – really unbelievable how intuitive he was. Daren couldn't make up his mind about Tom, but the only thing he *was* sure about was that he really wanted to talk to him again, right now.

Daren finally came to the conclusion that he needed a new routine. To get his body healthy enough to ultimately make a full recovery from the ravages of the cancer he would need to establish better eating habits with healthier foods, follow a gradual but consistent exercise program, and adopt an even more positive mental outlook about everything. He was mindful that he had come a long way and was making progress with that third component, the mental attitude part, but he would try even harder now in that area to supplement those first two. They were the things his doctor had recommended, and he was finally deciding in his own mind that all of these things combined could make a significant difference in his health. Think, eat, and live healthy – those would be his new goals.

He was also going to have to face the dilemma of finding a new place to live. He only had a few more days left in the motel room before his money ran out. After that his prospects were uncertain.

When he heard the knocking on his door this time it sounded unlike that of either the prophet or Lloyd, and again he didn't recognize the signature of the knocks. But when he opened the door he recognized the man immediately.

"Hi Daren," the man greeted him, "I hope I didn't catch you at a bad time. Remember me, Lane Darnell from Mammoth Apparel? Is now a good time to ask you about something?"

"Sure," Daren said, "now is as good a time as any other time. Won't you come in?"

Lane entered the room and sat down, "You're not so easy to find, you know. I finally thought to ask Austin's father about where I might find you, and fortunately he knew."

"Oh yeah," Daren said, "I no longer have a phone, and I was recently forced to move out of the house I had been renting, so I don't yet have a permanent address. I plan to be out of this tiny room in only a matter of days, but I don't know where I'll end up just yet."

"Well, what I came to ask you is whether or not you'd be interested in a job. You're presently not working, is that correct?"

"That's right. I was working for Sinclair Technologies, testing electronic circuits. I had been there for eight years before they let me go, and it was a fairly decent job. My former supervisor, Will Haft, will probably tell you that I was laid off because of the slump in the economy. That's the way Will is. He's one of the nicest guys I've ever known, and he'll do just about anything to protect one of his crew. But the truth is that I was fired. They had to let me go because of my attitude. I had such a chip on my shoulder, and looking back I can't even say exactly why. I wasn't getting along at all well with fellow employees, and my work output was suffering towards the end. I've changed a lot of things in my life in the short time since, but anyway, that's the *real* reason I lost my job. I realize that's not exactly what you wanted to hear, but it is the truth."

Lane looked about the tiny room, and Daren could sense his surprise at the meager accommodations.

"Well, I do appreciate your honesty. But I don't really care too much about the past. What I know about you is just what I've seen, that you can put together a solid and convincing presentation, and that your demonstrated creativity and commercial intuition are valuable assets to my world. I want you to consider joining my team. We can use your kind of talent. Have you seen or heard much in the local news within the last couple of days?"

"No, I haven't at all. I don't own a television or a computer, or even a radio for that matter. Why?"

"Since one of the local TV stations showed an interest in Austin's story our company's been getting quite a bit of positive publicity for our part, just as you had projected we would in your presentation. And even though it's only been a matter of days, we've already started noticing a rise in our sales. It's anybody's guess just how far that will ultimately go before things cool back down, but right now it's looking promising. It shouldn't be too long before we're ahead on the whole deal."

"I'd love to accept your job offer, Lane, but I have terminal cancer. It's in remission right now and I feel pretty good sometimes, but according to the cancer specialist I'm not expected to live even one more year. I might survive half that long if I'm lucky. Unlike Austin's condition, mine is in an advanced stage and medically un-curable at this point."

"I'm very sorry to hear that, Daren," Lane said, looking stunned. "I wish there was some way that I could help you with it. I lost my cousin to prostate cancer only two years ago. It was a very difficult time for our families. Robby and I were next-door neighbors while growing up and we ran around together a lot, went to the same school, and were probably as close as a lot of twins are. I'm sure that whole ordeal influenced my decision concerning Austin Price. His situation really touched a nerve with me. Of course, that turned out to be the right decision."

"Yes, it looks like it sure was, in more ways than we can know," Daren commented.

"So anyway, if you think you'd be up to it, health-wise I mean, we'd sure love to have you on our team, at least until your condition starts getting worse if that happens. It's a salaried position, and your title would be 'Marketing Specialist', with a sixty thousand annual salary. Paychecks are issued weekly. I'm not sure exactly how the employee benefits that include the insurance enrollment would work given your pre-existing cancer, but we can cross that bridge when we get to it. It's really a great company to work for. Would you like to at least think it over and maybe let me know later?"

"I guess I don't need to think about it too much. I've got nothing else going on right now, and I'm trying to stay hopeful about beating this disease. I might just survive it, you know. That job you're describing sounds interesting. I think I'd enjoy it. When would I start?"

Lane smiled, "You met Nancy and Keith from my team at your presentation. They've started putting together a full pager for the fall issue in one of the regular fashion magazines. If you could be in the studio around eight o'clock Monday morning, they will fill you in on what they've been developing, and you might have some good input on it. That project is really still in the brain storming stage, but it has to get done and submitted pretty soon if it's going to be on schedule with that magazine. I'll get your paperwork over to Personnel tomorrow morning first thing. Welcome aboard!"

Chapter 6

The Truth is Revealed

◊

When Amy checked her mailbox she found the only piece of mail in it was a card-size envelope with no return address. Her curiosity wouldn't allow her to wait until later to open it.

It was the little card that Daren had made. She immediately recognized his comic-style artwork. Her first inclination was to throw it away without even bothering to read it or look very closely at it, and she was about to drop it into the wastebasket when she suddenly decided against doing so. Her curiosity wouldn't let her just toss it without at least first taking a look.

On the front flap was a depiction of a cute puppy with sad eyes and its tail between its legs holding one paw on a little girl's knee. On the floor at the little girl's feet was a doll that had been visibly chewed on by the little puppy. The caption below it said, "How can I ever say I'm sorry?"

When she opened the flap she read Daren's hand-written words, "People really can change. They can throw away their old bad disposition and adopt a new positive one. They can do it permanently." The card was simply signed, "Daren".

Part of her wanted to believe what was written and illustrated on that card, and part of her wanted to just pitch it into the wastebasket as she had originally intended and simply forget all about it. She finally slipped it into her purse. She could figure it out later she decided, whether to keep it or discard it, when she had more time to think. Right now she was on her way to a meeting.

It was a support group of divorced and mostly abused women. All had been victims of either domestic violence or some other kind of spousal abuse. There were eight ladies in the group besides the counselor, and they met every Wednesday morning for an hour and a half therapeutic session of sharing and talking about their own personal struggles. Amy had been attending the meetings religiously for a little over two months, hoping it would help her deal with her emotional pain.

"Amy, what might you have to share with us this morning?" Mrs. Crowley, the counselor asked, calling on Amy first in the line of ladies seated in a semi-circle facing the counselor's chair, after noticing that she appeared to be preoccupied with something.

"I don't know," responded Amy, "I don't know what to think about certain things anymore, I guess."

"What do you mean specifically? What kinds of things? Are you referring to something concerning your relationship with your ex-husband, or maybe some other relationship? Is this anything you'd like to expound upon here in our group today?"

"I don't know really. I mean, what should I do if my ex-husband has been coming around wanting to fix all of the mistakes he's ever made in his past? Do I give him the chance – see where his intensions take him, or do I stand up firm like I've promised myself I would finally do? I just hate making the same old mistake I made a thousand times before and fall for his tricks all over again where I kept giving him the benefit of the doubt and then later regretted it. How can I know if he's *really* changed his ways? What should I do?"

Mrs. Crowley just seemed to stare at Amy for a moment. She didn't seem to have an answer for her.

"That's a very good question. Anyone else want to address that one?"

The new lady in the group appeared eager to offer her own perspective and she spoke up quickly, "Hi everyone, my name is Lisa, and I'm new to this group. I think in some ways I might be able to relate closely with Amy's dilemma. My ex-husband had the worst temper of anyone I've ever known, and he would get violent with me sometimes. Maybe Amy's ex isn't violent like mine, I wouldn't know. But Lloyd is a really big guy, and he can really hurt people when he goes into a rage. We were high school sweethearts when I was a cheerleader and he was a star player on our football team. We got married right after graduation. Well, I put up with his abuses for years, and

66

we had a son together. I eventually made the hard decision to leave Lloyd, and take my son, and I finally got a restraining order against him.

"Then my son was diagnosed with Leukemia, and all of our lives changed completely. Lloyd started wanting to make up for all that he had done, and he became basically obsessed with that. As much as I still loved him, I just didn't feel comfortable trusting him with a second chance.

"And then this guy showed up at my house saying that he had met Lloyd, and that somehow he knew all about us – he knew things about Lloyd, about me, and about our son's illness. It was strange how he knew everything that he knew, but he kept talking about trying to help us all mend our broken lives. He was very optimistic sounding. I liked hearing what he had to say, even though common sense should have made me more suspicious I guess. I realize that sometimes I'm a little naïve about things.

"Anyway, the man said that he had terminal cancer, too, and that the one thing he wanted to do more than anything else before it would be too late would be to repair all of the pain that he had caused his ex-wife. His desperation about doing that was so much like Lloyd's. He seemed so sincere about everything, you know? I was moved enough by his inspirational story of trying to change himself for the better that I decided to give Lloyd a second chance, at least to get back to being on speaking terms with him for a while, I mean, and let him continue his relationship with his son.

"And so I got the restraining order lifted, and Lloyd seemed very willing to get help with his anger management. So far he's been a changed man. He's been managing his temper amazingly well lately. I've noticed a world of difference, and I pray it will last.

"But what really caused me to believe in miracles was that this man somehow managed to convince a clothing retailer to pay for a medical procedure that we believe will save my son's life, which we couldn't find any other way to pay for. So I guess it's fair to say that this man saved my son's life, and he also saved our family. What kind of man would go to such lengths to do all of that? I really hope that his ex-wife eventually learns what kind of man he is now. I am now a believer in second chances."

Amy could no longer hide the tears that had been welling up in her eyes, but she was still able to keep a degree of composure, "Thanks, Lisa," she said, "That does help me and I appreciate hearing your story. Would you happen to remember that man's name?"

Lisa nodded, "Yes, he said his name is Daren – Daren McBride I think he said."

Amy's emotions suddenly gushed uncontrollably.

It was three days later when Amy finally decided to go to Daren's house and knock on his door. She was surprised that Daren's former landlord, Mr. Harrington answered the door.

"Hi Mr. Harrington. I came by hoping to talk to Daren," she said. "Does he no longer live here?"

"Oh, no Amy, he moved out about two weeks ago. I moved into this house shortly after the divorce from my ex-wife was finalized and she got the home we were living in together. A dose of karma, I suppose. So I take it that he didn't give you a forwarding address either, huh?"

"No, he didn't. He probably tried to a few times, but I was just so…"

"Well, when you *do* finally catch up with him, please relay my sincerest apology for the kind of landlord I was with him. I forced him out of the house for being late with his payment three times in a row, which I was legally entitled to do in accordance with our lease agreement. But I was so wrong to do that. Daren was having some financial difficulties towards the end and I knew that, yet I cut him no slack. Even after all those months when he paid on time like clockwork, I cut him no slack when he needed some slack. And even when his illness started getting worse, I still wouldn't cut him any slack on his rent. I'll tell you something, Amy, when Daren moved out, do you know what he did when he moved out?"

"No, I wouldn't have a clue, Mr. Harrington. What did Daren do?"

"Well, he cleaned this place up inside and out, cleaner than I've ever seen it. I found it in tip-top condition, with the yard freshly mowed and everything when I inspected it after he was gone. None of my other tenants have ever done that. He didn't even want his deposit back, which he was absolutely entitled to. Now I don't know where he is, and I want to give him that deposit money back. Something in me changed after he moved out of this house, and now I want more than anything to apologize for being such a jerk with him. Will you tell him that for me, Amy, when you find him?"

"I promise I will, Mr. Harrington, just as soon as I find him. There's been quite a lot of that apologizing going on lately. Maybe not so much apology *accepting* when there should be, but certainly an awful lot of apologizing."

Daren was really looking forward to starting his new job. In a way it was a new kind of beginning for him. With that to look forward to he felt empowered to find a nice apartment to rent. He would soon have the resources for things like that, and there would be no need now to even think about living the life of a homeless bum as he had begun to envision more frequently in his future.

He had already started his new routine. Daily exercise entailed walking about half a mile each day while he was feeling good enough to do it. He was following his doctor's recommendation about avoiding strenuous exertion while still managing to get *some* exercise. And his eating habits had changed considerably as well. He started buying more fruits and vegetables, fresh fish, and whole grains at the supermarket. Those things replaced the beer, chips, and frozen ready foods that he had been more accustomed to buying whenever he went grocery shopping. He was now ever more determined about turning his life around for the better, in every way he could think to do it. And he was beginning to notice improvements in the way he felt, and in the amount of energy he suddenly always seemed to have now.

His first day on the new job turned out to be the most enjoyable workday of his life as far as he could remember. Everything about it was purely fun for him. The other team members were easy to work with. The project was interesting. His own input was purely creative. Daren was taking to this like a duck takes to water.

The only thing missing in Daren's life at the moment, for a nearly perfect life in almost every way in accordance with his new perspective on things, was Amy. At one point he even considered attending her church, and actually making it a routine part of his Sunday mornings until he found some way to show her that he was a new man now. But almost as soon as he got that idea he dismissed it. Amy had been about as clear as a person should ever have to be about anything, and if he had learned anything at all about respecting other people, if he had *really* changed into a new man, he should honor her wishes. It would certainly be a first for him.

When he found the available apartment he liked within a five-minute drive of his new place of work, it didn't take him very long at all to move in with his limited amount of possessions. He simply unrolled his sleeping bag on the floor, opened his shaving kit on the countertop in the bathroom, hung a bath towel on the towel rack with a bar of soap next to the vanity basin, hung his finer clothing on hangers in the bedroom closet and the task was basically done.

The following day he purchased two lawn chairs for his living room for less than twenty dollars each and a small folding table to set his writing pad on. He had recently learned to be content with a minimum of furnishings.

The apartment came furnished with an electric range and a refrigerator, so those were two useful items he wouldn't have to bother with. And he found several cook pots and a frying pan, some drinking glasses, bowls, plates, and a dozen eating utensils at a local thrift store, all for ten dollars. The only other thing he decided to buy, besides the cell phone at the request of his new employer, was a vacuum cleaner for the carpet and a wastebasket for his trash. He was bent on keeping his life as simple as possible, at least for now.

It had been several weeks now since he'd contemplated suicide. It was hard for him now to even imagine doing something like that, but a lot had certainly changed in his world over those several weeks.

Chapter 7

A Change Confirmed

◊

He got off work at four o'clock in the afternoon and was driving home when he spotted the Ford Bronco parked on a side street with a "for sale" sign on its window. He decided to stop and investigate. He had long wanted a Bronco, for camping and fishing trips. For some reason he liked the way the Broncos looked compared with other popular 4x4 vehicles.

The sign on the driver's side window gave a phone number, and showed a price of $2,500.00 "Or best offer". It showed it as a 1990 model, noting that it only had 97,000 miles on its original engine. A quick inspection around the outside of the vehicle, plus a peek through the window at the interior showed it to be in very good condition. It had apparently been well maintained, probably a one-owner vehicle.

Daren didn't write down the phone number, but he repeated it over and over again in his head to memorize it. He decided that when he got home he would give the owner a call. He'd been thinking a lot lately about taking some camping/fishing trips to the nearby mountains, and this rugged Ford seemed ideal for that. His own car, a 2005 Buick Park Avenue – the last year of production for the Park Avenue – was really too much of a town car for those kinds of adventures up into the mountains, he thought.

Only about five or six blocks away from that side street where he'd stopped to look at the Bronco Daren was entering an intersection right after the light had changed to green. The traffic was getting noticeably heavier as more and more people were starting to leave from work, and out of the corner of his eye Daren saw the heavy truck approaching from the right cross street that had not stopped for the red light.

Everything suddenly seemed to slow way down in his perception of things around him. He heard himself yelling out, "Oh no, that truck isn't stopping!" But he was completely helpless to avoid being struck by the large truck, and all he could do was let the air bag slam against him and ride out the violent sideways shove from the heavier vehicle.

The impact was loud with breaking glass and the crunching of sheet metal, and when it was over he found himself suspended upside down in his seatbelt, with his crumpled car on its side on the lawn of a professional complex of buildings, at least twenty yards from the edge of the road.

In the brief duration of the collision Daren saw his life flashing before him. He thought it would all be over in a blink of an eye, but here he was, seemingly unhurt in his smashed car, trying to wiggle his way out of the seat belt and through the broken side window in a door that was stuck shut. Simultaneously he heard a side door opening and closing on the truck that had crashed into his car. It was less than fifty feet away.

The man came quickly over to help him out of his car.

"Are you injured, Sir?" the approaching man asked with genuinely sounding concern.

"No, I don't think I'm hurt at all. How about you?"

"I'm fine. That heavy truck didn't smash up like your car did – just some bumper damage is all it looks like. I am so sorry for this! I don't know how I could have missed that red light. I've been driving since I was sixteen – that's eight years ago, and I've never ever had a ticket of any kind, or been involved in any auto accidents in my entire life. But I clearly had a brain glitch here, didn't I? Thank God you're not mangled or killed. You sure you're not just in shock maybe? Sometimes people don't feel the really bad injuries right away, like hard-to-see internal injuries and cuts."

Daren glanced down to inspect himself, opened and closed his hands, moved his arms, and stood straight up to test his legs. He noticed a scrape on the back of his left hand, but it was only skin deep. Under his right knee his leg was a little bit sore. He'd probably have a bruise there tomorrow. But other than a few minor things like that he felt fine.

"No," he said, "I really do believe I'm okay. The car sure is a mess, but I must have some sort of guardian angel watching over me."

The driver of the truck shook his head, "Wow, it is hard to believe that anyone could walk away from such a wreck without at least a broken arm or concussion to the head, or *something*. That's just a miracle."

"I guess I'll just be grateful about it," Daren extended his right hand for a handshake, "I'm Daren, by the way. Daren McBride."

The young truck driver paused, surprised that the survivor of a smashed up car would be in a greeting kind of a mood. He slowly extended his own hand and shook Daren's, "My name is Kyle Hintz. You already know that I'm the driver of the truck that, um, you know, made this mess," he pointed towards the logo on the side of the truck with the company name, *Hendricks Rock & Gravel*.

"Been driving for that company very long?"

"Almost three months now. Great company to work for – pays really well. My wife and I have a two-year-old daughter and I had been unemployed for about four months when Mr. Hendricks hired me as a driver. That job was a godsend for us, because we were able to finally start paying some bills we'd been late on. But unfortunately, I won't be working for that company any longer."

"Why is that?"

"Well, his new company policy is to let any driver go after even one accident. It used to be *two* accidents and a driver would be gone, but two of the company trucks have been in accidents in just the last three years, besides this one today. The insurance rates for the company are getting pretty high so I guess the new rule about accidents makes sense as far as that goes."

"Not if it creates unnecessary or unreasonable hardships for good people, it doesn't," Daren said sympathetically. "Accidents like this happen to the best of us, and like you said, you've been an excellent driver with a perfect driving record. It seems like that should count for something."

"I know, but I sure messed up this time. Look at your car. I nearly killed you. I can't believe I nearly got someone killed today like this!"

"But you didn't kill or injure anyone, and that's ultimately what's really important. You sure wouldn't want to let something like this get you down. Learn from it, yes, and then get on with your life."

It was only a few minutes later that the police arrived on the scene and made an accident report. A tow truck was summoned to haul Daren's wreck to a wrecking yard. Kyle offered to drive him on home, even though it was against company policy to veer off the route like that or to transport anyone besides company employees in the truck, but company policy suddenly didn't seem so important under the circumstances. Daren accepted the ride home.

Later that evening Daren got a call on his new cell phone from Chuck Hendricks, Kyle's employer and the owner of the rock and gravel company he drove for. He explained that he'd gotten Daren's number from the police report, and he asked right away if Daren had already filed a claim with his company's insurance carrier. Daren explained that he had not yet done that.

"Well then, if you'd rather settle directly with me for a

potentially faster and more suitable settlement than you might expect from an insurance company's claims adjuster, I will treat you as fairly as I possibly can," said Chuck. "You see, a third insurance loss in this three-year period, which is what this one would be for my company, will most likely result in the carrier non-renewing our insurance in December. We'd have to be set up with a high-risk plan on our commercial auto insurance after that, and it would probably cost us about twice as much. You don't want to know how much we pay even for the business auto insurance we have now, and doubling that would be... I'll just say that if I can possibly pay this one out of pocket I believe it will be better for my company in the long run."

"What exactly did you have in mind?"

"Okay, I looked up the blue book value of your 2005 Buick, and it was worth seventy-five hundred dollars in excellent condition. My understanding is that you weren't badly injured, but you might go see a doctor anyway if you haven't already, just to be on the safe side. Assuming nothing major turns up there, I'd go a thousand to cover the doctor visits, plus another five hundred to cover the towing company's charges, and whatever's left over you could keep for your own inconvenience. If this is a fair offer in your view, I'll drive over to your place as soon as you like and give you a check for the nine thousand dollars. Of course, I would need for you to sign something to release me on all further liability if I do that, and you'd have to agree not to make any insurance claims."

"It's a fair enough offer probably, but I have an even better idea. How about you pay me just the seventy-five hundred that my car was worth, I won't make any insurance claims, and you keep Kyle on as your employee, at least through the end of this year if not indefinitely? He said he's got a clean driving record not counting what happened today, but that your company has a new policy about letting drivers go after their first accident."

"He's right about our new policy. We had to set down a stricter rule on it after two of our trucks were involved in accidents in such a short amount of time. But Kyle is definitely one of my best guys, and I sure hate to let him go. I'd never even think of doing that if it weren't for our new company policy, but we simply had to take action on this. What happened today merely underscores the importance of cracking down on the problem."

"I can understand that, but Kyle and his family really need that paycheck, Mr. Hendricks," Daren insisted. "If you'll tweak your company's policy just a little and keep Kyle on, I'll take your seventy-five hundred and I'll sign whatever you want me to sign."

The very next day Daren contacted the man who owned the Ford Bronco that he'd seen for sale, and he ended up buying it from him. He decided to pay him the full asking price, even knowing full well that he could have beat him down on it, probably down to as low as two thousand dollars. There was a time not so awfully long ago Daren realized when he would have delighted in chiseling the seller down just as far as he possibly could, then later brag to everyone about how he'd successfully squeezed "blood from a turnip". But his whole perspective about this sort of thing had changed lately.

"I don't have any idea what kind of 'best offer' you

would end up taking for this Bronco, Sir, but in my opinion it's well worth the twenty-five hundred you're asking, I *have* the twenty-five hundred, and with my medical condition I may not even live long enough to fully enjoy any sort of difference I might have saved on the deal, assuming I'd managed to get you to take less. Besides, yesterday I got my full price for my Buick. Today it's your turn."

Daren could see the relief in the man's eyes, and he had a sense that he desperately needed that money. Were it not for that it was doubtful the man would be selling the vehicle at any price he guessed, considering the care that it had obviously received since it was new.

Now that he had what he considered to be the perfect camping vehicle, Daren decided to plan out a camping and fishing trip before it would be too late for him to do anything like that. He would need some camp gear – nothing fancy, but a few basic items like a tent, some fishing tackle, a folding chair, a picnic cooler, a mess kit for camp cooking, etc.

A two or three day nature outing could only be good for his health he believed, and if he planned it for an upcoming holiday weekend he wouldn't even have to take any time off from work. He enjoyed the new job too much to want to take any time off from it yet. But he knew of a remote lake that he hadn't been to in years, and he was itching to visit the area again.

They had a sale on folding camp chairs at the local sporting goods store: two chairs for the price of one, and even that two-for-one price was discounted from the regular one-chair price.

Buying two chairs instead of one caused Daren to think about Amy, as if he would be buying that extra chair for *her* to sit in, as if she would be camping out there at the lake with him, even though he knew that wasn't going to happen. But the idea was for some reason planted in his brain, and it started to bring on a powerful sense of loneliness all of a sudden – the same kind of feeling that he had only recently been able to shake. In reality that extra camp chair could be useful, he realized, for keeping some of his smaller gear off of the possibly muddy ground.

The time seemed to pass by much too quickly for a man whose life would be over soon. Everything that had happened recently and with the way he saw things now, he wasn't at all eager for any of it to end anytime soon.

When the time came to start packing for the camp and fishing trip, he started making a list of everything he wanted to take. One of the first things he thought of to put on the list was his revolver – the same Smith & Wesson he very nearly used to put an end to his own existence only weeks earlier. It was one of his few personal possessions that he had managed to hang onto. The purpose for having the gun with him out in the woods was primarily for emergency last-resort defense against any overly aggressive wild animals like bears. The gun, a 41 Magnum, had gone with him on a number of hiking/camping trips in years past, and it had always provided him with a better sense of security than did going into wild places without it.

It suddenly occurred to him that he was actually concerned now about his own security and well being – he was going to pack the gun along to protect himself from possible danger. This was quite a contrast from the hopelessness he had entertained during his moments of deepest despair when he had seriously planned on ending his life.

Thinking of that along with his consciously charitable dealings with other people over the past few days provided him the confirmation that he had been looking for, the confirmation that he had indeed changed. He had completely changed his outlook on life. He found himself really wanting to live, there was no question in his mind about it now, and now he would *fight* to live. If the cancer ultimately killed him, then at least he would die fighting.

Chapter 8

Some Things Are Not What They Seem

◊

Though Daren hadn't been to the lake in years, he found that it was still pretty much exactly the way he had remembered it. On the way out there he picked up two Styrofoam cartons of earthworms from a little bait and tackle shop just outside of town that had traditionally opened for business fairly early in the morning to cater to guys who, like Daren, would invariably find themselves thinking about the fish bait at the very last minute.

He arrived early enough to be the first and only person at the lake, and he had his pick of the best camp spots along the shoreline. It didn't take him very long at all to get his tent pitched on relatively level ground and his campsite set up for comfort and convenience on his favorite part of the lake.

There was a nice ring of rocks already in position around a well-used fire pit on the small patch of sandy beach, and he opened up his two chairs close to this fire pit and facing the water where he could sit with his fishing rod in his hand and feel the warmth of the fire against his back. He set his cooler full of ice and assorted beverages next to his chair.

He spent maybe twenty minutes gathering dead branches from the surrounding woods for firewood, and he made a neat stack within arm's reach of the fire pit. It wasn't long at all until he was able to sit down with his fishing pole baited and cast, where he could relax and enjoy the natural scenery, and wait for a fish to bite.

Not even a half hour had gone by from the time he got himself settled in before a noisy older pickup truck arrived and drove into one of the nearby open campsites along the lakeshore where it immediately parked. After the engine shut off a man and a small boy, presumably his son emerged from the vehicle's cab, and they made a quick inspection of the area. When the man noticed Daren, he waved, and Daren waved back and smiled, noticing the excitement expressed by the little boy.

"Are the fish hungry today?" the man asked loud enough for Daren to hear.

"Too early to tell. I just got here less than an hour ago myself. No bites yet, but it's still early."

"I brought my son out here for his first ever campout, and I guess this is his first real fishing trip, too."

"How old is your son?"

"Cole just turned five last month."

"He looks big for five. He'll love this lake. It's a great place for a kid to spend his first campout, and the fishing is usually really good here."

"What are you using for bait?"

"Worms. What about you guys?"

"We brought a jar of salmon eggs, plus I have my fly rod with me, and a package of cheap store-bought flies. I don't have too much faith in those, but it was kind of a last-minute decision, you know?"

"I understand how that is. Well, you're welcome to one of these cartons of worms if you want to give them a try. I probably bought too many for just me. I've caught a lot of fish out of this lake in years past, but never on anything besides worms."

"Thanks. Just might take you up on that offer after a while. We'll see how it goes with what we've got here first, though."

Not an awful lot of dialogue was exchanged between them for the next several hours while the man and his son were busy getting their own camp set up and focusing on their own activities. But it didn't take Daren very long to catch three pan-size trout, and when he learned that his camp neighbors hadn't caught any all day long he gave them two of his fish.

The next morning Daren was up and about his camp, getting a fire going for brewing his morning coffee, before his neighbors made their first appearance of the day outside their tent.

He looked into the surrounding trees and took a deep breath of the fresh morning air. His days seemed much more important to him now than in the past, and he didn't want to miss even one sunrise if he could avoid doing so.

Everything seemed to impact his senses so much more out here in this natural setting than he was used to in town, he thought as he watched the foot-thick blanket of fog hugging the glassy still surface of the lake. It was quiet out here, other than the sound of four ducks on the far edge of the lake and a distant crow cawing, and he marveled at the beauty of it all. For a moment at least, he wondered why he would ever want to go back to his life in the city.

When the camp neighbors finally emerged from their tent and stretched their legs, he offered a cup of hot coffee to the man, and a cup of hot cocoa to the boy, since his fire was already crackling hot. They both heartily accepted and walked over to his site for a friendly visit.

Daren learned some things about the man. His name was Johnny Kincaid, and he worked as a city garbage truck driver/operator. He shared some interesting stories about the various treasures he had salvaged from both residential and commercial trash bins over the years, and Daren suddenly found the whole concept of "dumpster diving" fascinating.

"I want to try that someday," he said. "I want to go rummaging through peoples' trash barrels just to see what sort of cool things I might find."

"You'd probably be amazed at what some people throw away. Those things I mentioned were just *some* of what I've recovered – a list would go on and on. I've sold things on eBay that I've rescued from trash, and in some cases got a pretty penny for the stuff. That's how I sold that antique hurricane lantern I told you about. The highest bid was sixty dollars. But people do that, they throw their stuff away when it's old looking, maybe needs a little repair, or just plain dusty from sitting on a shelf."

After they had finished their hot drinks and talked for maybe another ten minutes, the two returned to their own campsite and before long had their lines in the water. Daren also decided to bait up and cast his line. He had been fishing on the bottom with a weighted line the day before, but now wanted to try it with a bobber on his line.

He was about to take a seat in one of his camp chairs with his fishing rod in one hand and his cup full of steaming hot coffee in the other when something in the distance caught his attention, and he turned in that direction for a closer look. He strained to see what looked like a human figure at least two hundred yards away, apparently walking on the road leading to the lake. As the image came into slightly better view, he observed that the person was walking with a limp and apparently using a cane.

"No way!" he blurted out, as soon as he recognized the form. It was Tom, that old white haired bearded prophet. How did the old man make his way out here? This was at least an hour's drive from Daren's apartment! A minute later Tom had approached close enough to exchange greetings.

"How'd you know I would be here of all places, Tom, and how on earth did you even get here? Where's your ride? Don't tell me you *walked* all this way from town!"

"Happy to see you, too, Daren. How are the fish biting?"

"I barely just got my line cast. I'm trying it with a

bobber this time. We'll see how it works. Can I rig up a pole for you? You do like to fish, don't you?"

The old man shook his head, "I didn't even buy a fishing license. But that's not why I'm here."

"Why exactly *are* you out here, Tom? Have you got another job for me to do, or something like that?"

"No, my friend, I have no more missions to send you on. You've done everything you needed to do, and now my work is also done. That's what I came here to tell you."

"When I hadn't seen you for close to two weeks I started wondering if I was *ever* going to see you again, Tom. Glad to see you're alive and well. Here's a chair for you to take a rest in, you must be exhausted after that fifty mile hike!"

Daren cleared his gear out of the extra chair he'd brought so that Tom could sit in it, and Tom graciously sat down.

"Will you have something to drink? I've got plenty of bottled beer and a few bottles of ice-cold Ginger Ale. Or, if you'd rather have a cup of hot coffee, or tea, or cocoa?"

"You may remember that I don't drink alcohol, but one of those cold Ginger Ales certainly does sound good after that long trip out here."

Daren pulled a cold bottle from his cooler and twisted the cap off, then set it in the drink holder in the arm of his chair where it would be conveniently ready for Tom when he wanted it.

"Did I hear you correctly to say that I've fulfilled all of my obligations as far as you're concerned?"

"Indeed you have, Daren. You've completely changed your whole disposition, and you've even proved it to yourself. You have restored yourself to the person you were years ago, back to when you first met Amy. Now all my work as the catalyst concerning you has been concluded. Well, you'll need to stay on course with this. The change has to be permanent. But I have confidence in you, Daren. You have indeed changed."

There was a moment of dead silence while Daren tried to think of something to say, and about what it all meant, all of what Tom had told him. It was Tom who finally broke the silence just after Daren noticed his neighbors looking over at him and talking quietly with each other, as if deliberately trying to avoid being overheard.

"Your neighbors over there aren't catching anything, are they? Maybe they could use some of your worms. It'd be a shame if they ended up going home after this trip without that little boy catching at least one fish."

"Sometimes I get the feeling you're reading my mind, Tom. I'll take my extra carton of worms over there right now."

After Daren walked over and handed Johnny the box of worms, he glanced back to wave Tom over, to come and meet these good neighbors, but the old man was nowhere to be seen. Daren scanned the immediate surroundings of his camp trying to see where Tom might have wandered off – he couldn't have gotten far in that short span of time. But there was no sign of him at all, and Daren shook his head in disbelief, and with equal disappointment.

"That's what he always does - that crazy old man, he disappears whenever you're not watching him. And I could never figure out how he does it."

"Who is it you're talking about?" Johnny asked him

with a bewildered look on his face.

"That old man I was talking with a minute ago. His name is Tom. I've known him for only about a month or so. Sure never expected to see him way out here today, though. Crazy, isn't he? He *walked* out here all the way from town!"

"We were wondering who you were talking to over there, Daren. Not that we wanted to be nosy or anything, but we just couldn't see whoever you were talking to."

"I was talking with that old guy with the cane who was just... He was sitting in my extra camp chair by the fire pit just a minute ago."

"But that's why we got so curious. It looked like you were talking to an empty chair. We haven't seen anybody sitting in that chair."

Daren looked at the boy, and the boy had an uncomfortable look his eyes that he wanted to hide but couldn't, uncomfortably thinking Daren might be crazy.

"Sorry, Sir. There really was nobody over there besides you," the boy said bluntly and honestly in his youthful voice. "I'm really sorry to tell you, but..."

Daren turned again to look back at his camp, and he just seemed to stare in that direction for an instant as if he couldn't believe what he had been told. In another instant he rushed back to his own camp and picked up the bottle of Ginger Ale he had previously set in the holder for Tom. He held it up where he could look at it closely, and he saw that the bottle was completely full. Daren realized immediately that a man who had just walked a number of miles to some remote location would be incredibly thirsty. There would be no way that a man could stop for just a few minutes after such a journey and then move on without taking a long drink of *something*.

Suddenly just about everything about the little old prophet seemed implausible. The color of his eyes: it seemed unlikely that anyone in the world would have eyes of that exact same color. And the ways in which he had always just appeared as if out of thin air, and then similarly vanished into thin air: nobody can do that like ole Tom always did it. He had to have been a figure simply created in Daren's imagination without him even knowing it. And the old man seemed to always be reading Daren's mind.

The shock of this sudden new realization – the reality that Tom never really existed except within his own mind - it seemed to turn his whole world upside down, and it suddenly became so disorienting to him that he started breathing uncontrollably faster and faster, nervously searching his mind for answers that made any sense of it. He kept staring at that empty camp chair, and he started feeling dizzy. His vision was rapidly blurring.

He could hear some voices, they sounded distant. He thought he recognized one of them as his camp neighbor Johnny's voice. He seemed to be asking Daren if he was okay, and then Daren sensed a tone of stress in the voices he was hearing as if some kind of emergency was unfolding. The bright blue of the sky straight above him was the last thing Daren remembered seeing.

Chapter 9

Mending the Relationship

◊

He woke up in a hospital bed. Clueless as to why he was there, or even how he got there, he looked around the room for a nurse or anyone else to ask those questions to. He was especially surprised to see the only person in the room besides himself in that moment was his ex-wife, Amy, sitting in a chair not more than two feet from the edge of his bed. He closed his eyes for two seconds and then opened them again as if to find out if his brain was playing tricks on him. She was still there when his eyes opened again. When she noticed that he was awake, her face lit up and she immediately smiled.

"How do you feel?" she asked softly.

"Fine, I guess," he glanced to one side of the room and

then the other. "Why am I here? This place looks and smells like a hospital. How long have I been asleep?"

"You collapsed while you were out camping yesterday. You hit your head pretty hard when you fell, and you've been unconscious ever since. Some other people were camping nearby, a man and his son I was told. They drove you into town. They brought you here."

"How did *you* find out that I was here?"

"The hospital did a next-of-kin search, and my name eventually came up. I was so surprised when I got that call. I was worried sick! But I've been trying to find you for a while, Daren. You moved without telling me."

"Yes, I did, didn't I? Well, I just figured you'd had more than enough of me lately. That was the message I kept getting, so why keep bothering you? But I *am* very glad you're here right now. I'm really happy to see you, Amy. You have no idea."

She couldn't think of exactly what to say, or how to properly express what she was feeling at that moment, so she simply reached over and took his free hand in hers and held it.

"I'm a changed man, you know? I'm not quite such a jerk anymore, at least I try pretty hard not to be."

She struggled to hold back her tears, "I know. Now I *know* that you're the man I married, that same man I fell in love with all those years ago."

He looked in her eyes, then down at her delicate hands sandwiching his own. He couldn't have dreamt anything like this, he convinced himself. At least this *seemed* real enough.

"So, how long will they keep me here, do you think?"

She gently set his hand down by his side and grabbed a tissue to wipe her eyes with, "Probably not very long, since the cancer is still in remission. But Dr. Richards says it's coming back, and he will want to start monitoring everything more closely now. He wants you to understand that you may be back here sooner than you expect."

"As if they can do anything to help me with that at this point."

"But you know how doctors are. I guess whatever they say you need to do, you should probably do. But you did also get a concussion when you hit your head, and they've been monitoring that closely."

Daren looked into her eyes again with an intensity that made her feel a bit uncomfortable, "Will I get to see you again? I mean, when they release me out of here, can I come over sometimes? I've got so much to tell you about. I'm not sure what all is real in my life anymore and what is just an illusion, but I really need to talk to someone."

"I'm real, Daren McBride, I can promise you that much. And I'm not going to leave you this time – that is, as long as you don't go back to acting the way you were acting for a while, which didn't suit you at all. But I could never willingly give up the man I fell in love with, the man I'm looking at right now."

He searched for something to say in order to change the awkwardness of the conversation, anything at all that he hoped would help him keep his own eyes dry, "I have a really good job now, in marketing. I love the work, and the company people are great to work with."

She knew what he was trying to do. She hadn't forgotten that he always tried to avoid exceedingly emotional discussions whenever possible, because he never liked to let anyone see him cry. She just smiled and listened.

"I'll need someone to drive me back up to the lake so that I can retrieve the Ford Bronco, and all of my camping gear. Can you help me with that whenever you get some free time? I should be well enough to drive it home, or at least I feel well enough, anyway."

"Of course I will. I can do it tomorrow or as soon as the doctor says you're okay to leave, assuming my boss will let me have the time off.

"So, you're driving a Ford now? You always were talking about those Ford Broncos. Did you trade your Buick in on it?"

"No, that Ford is not exactly a new rig. But I needed another vehicle because the Buick was wrecked. A heavy gravel truck T-boned me in an intersection."

"Sorry to hear that. I remember how much you liked that car. You weren't injured, were you?"

"That was the miracle of it. Nobody sustained any more than a few bruises."

"Thank God."

"Exactly what I've been saying everyday since it happened."

When Daren called in to the office and explained to his boss everything that had happened, he was told to take all the time he needed to take care of his personal matters.

"We finally got that magazine spread submitted last week," Lane Darnell explained, "so now we can take a little breather before jumping into the next big project. Take whatever time you need right now.

"By the way," he made sure to mention before hanging up, "I spoke to Allan from accounting yesterday, and he wanted me to relay to you that the PR campaign funding that boy's medical procedure has apparently increased the company's sales revenues a full twenty percent this quarter already. And even more important is that the procedure is turning out to be very successful for the boy, I understand. So far it looks like it's curing his leukemia. Just thought you'd like to hear the latest on that."

When Daren and Amy returned to the lake where Daren had camped only a few days earlier, he found his campsite and all of his gear including the Bronco, tent, his revolver inside his tent, and even his two chairs still there and set up just as he'd had them, almost as if he'd never left, and everything appeared to be undisturbed. This was a Monday, and there were no other people at the lake now.

"I'm kind of surprised that a bear hasn't come into the camp and made a mess of everything," Daren said, visibly relieved as he inspected things.

"And you're lucky someone didn't steal your stuff," she commented, "especially the Bronco. That is a nice looking vehicle. It really does look just as well maintained as you described it."

Daren opened the lid on the camp cooler. Even though the ice had all melted and the bottled drinks were half submerged in the water, the water was still cold and it kept the drinks chilled. He grabbed a bottle of Ginger Ale, twisted the cap off and handed it to Amy, then picked up a bottle of beer for himself.

"We might as well drink to this good fortune," he said, and they sat down in the two camp chairs to enjoy the atmosphere while they sipped on their drinks.

This was more than he could have realistically hoped for, he thought, sharing this moment with Amy out here at this quiet lake. And he couldn't help but marvel at the irony of it - she was presently sitting in the camp chair that was the very thing that triggered his feelings of loneliness thinking about her right after he'd bought it.

"I see you're not lighting up a cigarette today," she said. "Apparently Dr. Richards managed to convince you to finally quit that habit, which is more than I was ever able to do. But I'm glad to see you're not smoking now."

He nodded, "A terminal illness can change a person's whole way of life I've noticed, that's for sure."

"I guess it would, yes. It's just too bad it sometimes takes a terminal illness to bring about positive changes."

"I still have a lot to do," he said, after taking a sip of beer. "Lots of making up for all I've done, or things I've failed to do that I *should* have done in my life. Funny how you start thinking about all this stuff when you know you're getting close to..."

He couldn't bear to finish the sentence, but he didn't need to. She knew what he was saying. She sat quietly and listened to him, understanding that he had a lot to talk about, that it was like a heavy burden he needed to unload from his shoulders.

"Amy, I want to spend the rest of my time on this planet helping people. You know, making peoples' lives somehow better, anyway that I am able to do that."

She finished her swallow and then set her drink in the cup holder in the arm of her chair, "I'm really happy to hear that, Daren, and to know now that you really mean it."

"Will you help me with it?"

She nodded, "Of course I will. You know I'd be happy to help you with that goal. It's not too hard to find people who need someone's help, in one way or another. A lot of people around us have a lot of needs, and so much of the time we don't even recognize it, or often care enough to help. I've been as guilty as anyone for failing to help those around me who've needed my help. But like you, now I want to do something about that."

They sat peacefully in their chairs for a few more minutes and just enjoyed each other's company and the natural scenery surrounding them without either of them saying a word. The weather was sunny with a clear sky but the temperature was only in the mid-70s, and this part of the day near the lake couldn't have been more pleasant. Finally Daren broke the silence.

"With the cancer in remission right now sometimes I feel like I'll wake up one morning and be completely cured. I've got a strong will to live now. I was able to find that within me, and it was quite a journey I must say.

"But if things take a turn for the worse and I start getting bad again, will you promise me something?"

Her mood became more serious, "Depends on what you're asking me to promise."

"I don't want to spend the last hours of my life in a hospital bed. I want you to bring me out here, where I can be in this beautiful place with this lake, the ducks, the trees, and the mountains."

"You mean like camping out here in a tent? That would seem awfully unpleasant. If you were suffering physically in a time like that, wouldn't you want to be where the trained professionals can help you with the pain?"

"But if I were truly at my life's *end*, what would anyone be able to do for me?"

She contemplated his request for a moment, and then agreed, "That's a good point. I guess we'll see how you feel about it when the time comes, *if* the time comes like that. But yes, if that's your final wish, I suppose."

As he looked at her sitting in the camp chair, spending this moment of her time with him, it was kind of hard to believe. He wouldn't have believed this would have been possible just a few weeks ago, and now he started feeling a little bit suspicious of this reality. When he started thinking more about it, it really did seem almost too good to possibly be true. She looked real enough, and everything in this moment seemed real enough right now, but then Tom also seemed to be real as he sat in that same camp chair only a few days earlier. Maybe the strange little old man *shouldn't* have seemed all that real, but he certainly did to Daren. And yet he was only a figure from Daren's imagination.

"What's wrong?" she said, sensing something was bothering him.

"My mind has been playing tricks on me quite a lot lately, Amy. Sometimes I'll see things that aren't really there – like people who don't even exist. But I'll think they do, until I find out later. This never happened to me before, but now I'm starting to worry."

"You know that I'm real," she tried to assure him, "that I'm really here with you right now, right?"

"I want to believe it, Amy. I *want* to. But what if I'm losing it?"

"Have you thought about going to see a psychiatrist about this?"

"You mean a *shrink*?"

"Hey, maybe someone like that can help you. Maybe there's a reason for all you've been experiencing, and maybe a 'shrink' can help you figure it out. What would you have to lose, anyway?"

"You wouldn't happen to know anyone in that line of work, would you? Anyone you know from church maybe?"

"In fact I did go see a psychologist a couple of times, right after we separated and before the divorce. Not that I really needed to necessarily, but I kept thinking it might help me with the depression I was feeling at the time. And he *was* able to help me to some extent with my issues, in spite of his reputation as being the most unorthodox, or sort of the oddball mental therapist in town. My friend, Sally, recommended him to me. He helped her, too.

"But more than a psychologist, a psychiatrist would be able to prescribe medication if needed, so maybe a psychiatrist would be the better option for you, although I'm no expert about these things. I've probably still got this guy's business card in my car somewhere, if you wanted to check with him first."

"I was the cause of your depression!" he acknowledged with a sudden sense of personal responsibility and remorse for what she had just disclosed.

"Not important now," she assured him, "I'm over all of that. It took me a long time to learn this, but I'm just now discovering how completely unimportant some things are in life, and how really important other things are. But I do now think it's important to let the past stay in the past as much as possible. The only thing that's important to me now is this particular moment we have together while it lasts, and that the only man I've ever loved has finally returned to his true character - the man I fell in love with has found himself again. So let's live for *that,* and try not to look back to the unpleasant times too much, okay?"

Chapter 10

Finding Out What Matters Most in Life

◊

When Daren had finished telling his whole story, the psychologist remained initially silent, took a sip from the water glass on his desk, and then cleared his throat before speaking.

"Wow," he expressed his marvel, "I've heard some remarkable stories during my career in the mental health field, but I'm pretty sure I've never heard anything quite like that. It is somewhat rare in my experience whenever someone totally changes his or her attitude about everything so completely like that. You always hear about these things, but…

"Would you mind if I included your story in a book I've been writing? I won't use your name if you preferred keeping that private unless you wanted me to, but I'd really like to add your fascinating story to my book. It's about some of the most fascinating conditions of the human mind that I've had the opportunity to witness in the course of my career. I could of course just describe whatever I discover about your experiences from my observation, but I'd actually rather have more details from your own perspective.

"I'll tell you what I'm willing to do if you're interested. You could have some sessions at no charge – and I believe I can help you – in exchange for your personal story. I'll need your help with all the details, but I love the story."

"I guess we could do that. I don't really mind whether you used my real name or not. How many free sessions are you talking about?" Daren was surprised by the degree to which this mental health professional was willing to bargain like a used car salesman. Suddenly he understood what Amy meant about him being something of an oddball.

"After hearing what I've heard of your story thus far I think I should be able to help you resolve your biggest issues with probably no more than three sessions, so how about we make it three one-hour sessions at no cost to you?"

"How about six one-hour sessions, just to be on the safe side?"

"After hearing just what you've told me this morning you shouldn't need that many, but I'll go four as long as you'll promise to help me with that part of my book, say at least ten minutes of each one-hour session. Would that work?"

"You have a deal. Now about this prophet I described,

um…"

"You were calling him 'Tom'."

"Right. What do you think that was all about? I mean, why would I invent someone like him?"

"Yes, so let's examine one possibility here. From what you've explained to me, you never *really* wanted to end your own life. You had a certain determination to finish what you'd set out to do that day, just like you said, but in your consciousness you never actually wanted to do it, so let's assume here just for a moment that your mind created Tom to mysteriously show up and talk you out of it. Maybe it was the way out that you needed. Otherwise I think it's reasonable to believe that you would have put that gun to your head and pulled the trigger, to fulfill an obligation to yourself you felt you had – simply about finishing what you'd started. Am I on the right track so far?"

"But Tom kept appearing periodically, even after I had completely decided against suicide."

The psychologist took another sip of water while he formulated his thoughts.

"Yes, because you were perhaps trying to resolve some other issues, and Tom had already proved capable of helping you with things that you didn't believe you could otherwise resolve alone."

"What you're saying then is that I needed this all-knowing prophet to just appear at the right moment and fix everything that needed to be fixed."

"Speculation on my part of course, and we should be careful making any assumptions with this sort of thing, but for a moment let's assume it's true. Down deep you believed you needed someone like Tom to guide you. Ultimately you handled all of these things on your own, because Tom was created in *your* mind. You guided *yourself* through those situations since there really never was in actuality this prophet named Tom. This is really an intriguing story from every perspective. Even though the prophet seemed to know everything, he never knew *anything* that you didn't already know, did he? You just didn't realize that at the time."

"And that's part of why I came to see you, because I'm never quite sure about what is real and what is not. How will I ever know for sure whether I'm losing my mind or not? Tom seemed very real, but obviously he wasn't. How can I know for certain that *anything* I see is real or merely imagined in my head?"

"I'm not so sure that any of us ever can. Ultimately we have only our senses to rely on for our brains to process information, and naturally our senses aren't always reliable. Sometimes our senses work as normal, and sometimes they don't.

"But as to whether or not you're losing your mind, I am inclined at this point to believe otherwise, although I would certainly recommend that you consult another mental health professional for a second opinion. I can give you a name of a practicing psychiatrist if you wish, someone I've known a long time and respect a lot.

"I base my opinion about this on several things. First, you stated that you don't have a history of mental illness, so I see no red flags to start with. Second, I've known a lot of people with schizophrenia, and you don't exhibit most, if any of the usual symptoms of schizophrenia. Third, according to your own story you have always had a very colorful imagination. And so did I while growing up. I was an only child who was quite introverted, and I created all kinds of imaginary friends to play with. To me they were all very real at the time, just as this Tom seemed real to you, until that pivotal moment you described at the lake. So, I can honestly say that I have some firsthand experience with the imaginary character syndrome.

"Understand also that your mental state is going to be affected to some degree by your physical condition, as is always the case with all of us – in your situation the cancer could have something to do with your mind playing little tricks on you from time to time. That sort of thing is not unheard of. You'll want to talk to your doctor about that, though, because it's completely out of my field. But I wouldn't expect you to see another imaginary person again anytime soon."

"Why's that?"

"Because now you're on to it. Now you'll be able to recognize something that doesn't seem totally real to you, recognize it as just an illusion, like when Tom mysteriously appeared and disappeared – those subtle clues. You'll be looking for those kinds of clues from now on."

"That's it then. I'm cured of my mental troubles and I shouldn't be needing those three other sessions."

"Not completely cured."

"What else is there?"

"You've got an enormous sense of guilt trapped inside that mind of yours. I also got that much from your story, and it's guilt over a lot of little things, but collectively they're considerable. We still need to clear that up."

"How can you possibly help me with my feelings of guilt, besides just telling me that whatever I feel guilty about is somehow not my fault?"

"First of all, I'm not a judge, and I wouldn't have any ideas about your innocence or culpability in any matters. So no, I won't tell you that anything's not your fault. What I *can* help you with are ways to resolve those feelings of guilt. I know what you need. You need resolution. You need to resolve those guilty feelings of yours, and be free of them."

"How can you help me find that 'resolution'?"

"You'll see soon enough how that will be. We'll go deeper into it in the next session. In the meantime, I'd recommend that you continue trying to help others just as you've been doing. Keep your creativity with that going. I'm sure you've noticed that it is quite rewarding and therapeutic for your state of mind. And you've already proved to yourself the degree to which a man can change his ways for the better. Most people never do that in their entire lives, but you have. By the way, Daren, do you consider yourself a religious man?"

"No, I don't, at least not in the traditional sense I guess I should say. I'm starting to view certain things in my life more spiritually now than I ever did before it seems, after learning about my terminal condition. It has forced me to think a lot about my own mortality."

"Well, the reason I asked that question is because those who adhere firmly to a religious faith of one kind or another often tend to deal much more easily with their own sense of guilt. Christians, for example, believe that their sins have been paid for with the blood of Christ. They know they've been forgiven for their transgressions, so they can let them go. They in turn find it much easier to forgive others, because for them it's all about forgiveness. The Christians I've worked with more often than not seemed so much at peace in this whole issue of guilt, in spite of their really messed up lives in some cases."

"Are you recommending that I start going to church on a regular basis?"

"Not specifically, no. Promoting religious doctrine of one variety or another is not normally associated with my profession. But this is something to think about, isn't it? You're actually searching for inner peace. Some people find that with religion," the psychologist looked at his watch. "We'll talk more about this when I see you next week. Right now we're out of time."

Daren had begun increasing the length of time and average distance of his walks around town each evening after work in his recently adopted routine, for the beneficial moderate exercise as well as to clear his mind of each day's meaningless details – the kind of meaningless details that life is too short for, he now believed. He told himself that he should have started this type of routine years ago. He kind of wanted to gradually step it up into a jogging routing, except that his doctor had warned him against too much exertion, and down deep he didn't really want to buck his doctor's advice. Two miles around town seemed to be about the right distance for him right now.

While walking past the bus station he noticed an old man searching for something in the dumpster in the back parking lot. The old man was obviously homeless, judging

108

by his wrinkled old clothing and his overall scruffy appearance. And he appeared to be preoccupied in his own little world, for the most part ignoring everyone and everything around him other than what he was focused on. When Daren looked closer, he suddenly remembered having seen the same old scruffy man about a year or so ago, in another part of town. And he had appeared to be scavenger hunting then as well.

It suddenly occurred to Daren that the imaginary prophet whom he called Tom had no doubt been inspired by seeing this same old man searching through the trash a year earlier. Daren had completely forgotten having seen him, but apparently his subconscious kept the man's character in his brain and created the prophet based on him. And the similarities were striking. This old man wore a beard, had almost white gray hair, and he also used a walking stick.

Daren approached the old man and tried to get his attention. It wasn't as easy to do as he had expected. The man was so deep into his own little world. Finally he looked up at Daren, and appeared to vaguely acknowledge him. Daren noticed his eyes – they were an unusual shade of green. While not exactly the same turquoise color of the imaginary prophet Tom's eyes, the inspiration for the unusual eye color was certainly obvious.

"Sir," Daren said for the third time until the man looked up, "are you looking for something that I might be able to help you find?"

The man mumbled something indiscernible, and then held up a cloth sack containing apparently some metal pots and glass jars, showing Daren his bag full of treasures from all of his dumpster diving.

Daren eventually learned from this old man that he spent some time off and on at the local homeless shelter, whenever harsh weather conditions made sleeping in the alleyways intolerable, he said. Daren also assumed, judging by the man's apparent lack of resources, that he probably went to the shelter whenever he got really, *really* hungry.

The old man appeared as if he didn't own possessions beyond whatever he'd found in the local dumpsters. But he didn't seem quite right mentally. When Daren offered to buy him something to eat he refused the offer, as if having anything to eat was unimportant. He insisted that he wasn't hungry right now.

When Daren asked the man for his name, the only answer he got was "Walt". Not Walt Smith, or Walt Jones, or Walt anything else, just Walt. There was definitely something mysterious about the old man, but Daren couldn't decide exactly what that was. And he couldn't seem to get the thought of the old homeless guy out of his head for the rest of the day. He had offered to help him, but even though the old homeless man appeared to need help desperately, he didn't seem to want any kind of help at all.

"Yes," Sarah Meade, the manager of the local homeless shelter nodded, "that's Walter Elliott. You've described him to a 'T'. Walt, as he prefers being called, marches to his own drum. Where did you see him?"

"In the Greyhound bus stop parking lot yesterday afternoon. He was digging through the trash bins in the back of the lot. I happened to be walking by and noticed him, but I remembered having seen him before."

"He's likely to turn up anywhere in the city," she said, "scavenger hunting in the garbage just like he's been doing for over fifteen years."

"Can he be helped?" Daren asked.

"In his own mind he doesn't admit that he needs any help from anyone, even though he has come to us a number of times and we've provided whatever immediate relief we could to help him survive along. If you were wondering whether or not his lifestyle could be changed or improved, I'd say probably not. He would have to want something else for himself, and he simply doesn't. Even if he did, I'm not sure that at his age…"

Daren shook his head, "It's a shame, isn't it?"

"There is not any shortage of lost souls in this city, Mr. McBride, and Walt is one of them. While there will always be that vast segment of every community that will try its damnedest to ignore those lost, often broken souls, there will also always be charitable folks among us who donate to organizations like this one whose entire purpose is to *not* ignore them. Walter Elliott is really a sort of misfit and will almost certainly never fit very well into mainstream society, and he will need us whether he wants to believe it or not. There were nights last winter when I'm sure he wouldn't have survived without the warm dry shelter and something to eat."

"I guess the question I should be asking is how might I be able to help with what you're doing here? I think this is exactly the kind of thing I need to become involved in."

"Our greatest challenge has been finding adequate

funding. The needs are always greater than the support. If you could somehow find a way to bring in more resources, maybe with some kind of fundraiser, that's what would make the most difference here."

On his way out of Sarah's office Daren noticed a vaguely familiar face donning an apron and entering the cafeteria kitchen. The man didn't look much older than about twenty-five, but he obviously hadn't shaved in a couple of days and he looked older. When he saw Daren he gave an angry stare. Daren couldn't remember where he'd seen the man before, but he felt certain that he had.

He felt an immediate impulse to confront the man and inquire as to the source of his apparent disapproval, but quickly decided against doing so. Daren had more important things on his mind at the moment than a distracting confrontation, and besides, the seemingly angry young man may have simply been having a bad day. He thought no more about the man's icy stare for the remainder of the day.

Daren suddenly had a new project to occupy his last days – he would concentrate his focus on finding some way to raise money for the homeless shelter. Later on in the evening when he called Amy on her cell phone he explained his newfound cause with enthusiasm, and she offered her own encouragement.

"How will you raise the money for the shelter?" she asked him with genuine interest.

"I haven't thought of any fancier idea yet than simply knocking on doors and explaining the need to the people I meet."

There was a pause in the conversation, and he almost

wondered if her cell phone's battery had died for a moment. But her eventual response assured him that she'd been quietly thinking.

"You'll have a lot of doors slammed in your face in this town you know, but you've always had that tenacious element in your character, Daren. I sure wouldn't want to be betting against your success."

"If you can think of a potentially more productive plan of action, I'd love to hear it."

"I've never given thought to it before, I'm kind of ashamed to admit. It is such a noble, and totally important cause. I was just thinking, I'd like to help you with it if you'd like me to."

"I'd love to have your help with this, Amy. You know, throughout my entire life I never really found any purpose that mattered as much to me as this one, until now. I just wish I'd been involved with things like this a long time ago."

"Never too late, my dear, as long as you're still able to do something like this," she reminded him.

Chapter 11

There is No Escape
From One's Own Past

◊

Daren and Amy both had the coming Saturday off from work at their respective jobs, and they agreed to meet at her apartment at eight o'clock in the morning before going out into neighborhoods together with their fund raising effort. After a cup of coffee and donning shirts with the homeless shelter's logo, they started their walk with clipboards in hand at one end of a long residential street, and knocked on first one door and then another, and presented their fund-raising pitch to everyone who answered a door.

The person who answered the door at the first house was a tired looking middle-aged woman still in her pajamas who seemed annoyed by their visit. In spite of Daren's inspirational speech she could not be persuaded to donate even a single dollar to the cause.

Nobody answered the door at either of the next two consecutive houses, but the door of the fourth house was answered by a sharply dressed woman who patiently listened to Daren's pitch, returned Amy's smile, and then promptly wrote a check payable to the homeless shelter for one-hundred dollars. "Yes," she said, "this is indeed a worthy cause, and I admire the two of you for getting involved with it." It was the largest single donation they would collect all day.

There were a few doors rudely slammed in their faces, but they expected some of that to happen. By lunchtime they had collected more than two hundred dollars for the shelter, and then they went back out again after eating sandwiches and knocked on another fifty or sixty doors. This kind of fundraising was exhausting as it involved a lot of walking and communicating with all kinds of people, but it was a rewarding experience and they both enjoyed it.

Before they had knocked on the last door for the day, Daren encountered the unpleasant distraction of a coughing fit that seemed to get worse and worse until they returned to the car and he was able to drink some water. The drink didn't make the coughing stop completely, but it helped. He couldn't help noticing that Amy had a worried look on her face.

"This happens from time to time," he said. "It's no fun at all when it does, but it usually doesn't last more than five or ten minutes."

"But you're feeling better now than you were feeling, at least for a while, right?"

He tried his best to go as long as he could between coughs, "I have my good days and my bad days, but it did seem like things were getting better for a while. I was starting to feel encouraged about things. I'm not so sure now, though."

"We might have to get you back in to see Dr. Richards right away. Despite your lack of confidence in conventional medicine, he might be able to help you at least feel a little bit better. That cough sure doesn't sound at all good."

"I've been putting that on hold for a while, because down deep I have this fear that once I go back into the hospital the next time, I'll never leave again – alive anyway. It's like I was telling you while we were out there at the lake, I just don't want to die in the hospital."

Amy's mood turned completely sober upon hearing those words. She nodded, appearing to be trying to fight back tears, "I understand," she mumbled, almost choking on her words, "and I won't push you into doing something you really don't want to do. That will have to be your decision, at least until things deteriorate to the point that... Well, hopefully it won't happen anytime soon."

Once inside the car his coughing subsided, and as they drove away they changed the subject. Lately Daren welcomed any distraction he could find from his medical condition, knowing that he'd have to face everything soon enough, anyway.

When they met with Sarah from the shelter Saturday

evening they excitedly presented her with the three hundred and sixty two dollars they had collected during their first day of fundraising.

"That's about forty meals we can provide to people who desperately need them," she informed them after making the quick calculation in her head. "Forty meals more than we could afford to provide otherwise. You two have no idea how grateful I feel right now."

"I think our entire community should be more grateful to you, Mrs. Meade," Amy said, "I believe I read it in the paper sometime last year that this is a true non-profit organization, and that you receive no compensation at all for your time and labor here."

Sarah shrugged her shoulders, "You have to love the work, as I do. I retired from a twenty-five year career with the city administration three years ago, and I receive a small pension from that so I'm able to put time into this. After that job ended I needed something to do with my time basically to keep me from going crazy, and then I found this. I realized immediately that I had to get involved, and I've never regretted doing so for one second. Now it consumes probably ninety percent of my waking hours, but it seems I can never leave the cause alone. It's just that I know there are so many people around who really can't care for themselves properly and they suffer. They routinely go hungry. I know that I can help them here."

"I plan to go back out again tomorrow," Daren said. "We'll see if I can raise another two or three hundred dollars. That's a lot of doors to knock on, but who knows?"

"That'd be great, if you can do it," Sarah commented.

"I wish I could go tomorrow, too," Amy said with a hint of disappointment in her voice, "but I'm scheduled to work all day on Sunday."

Daren nodded toward the bank deposit bag on the table in front of them, "If we could just recruit some more people into this fundraising effort, get them out knocking on doors all over town on a regular basis, then we could really do some good.

"Oh, just remembered," he continued, changing the subject, "that young man who works in the cafeteria with dark hair and close beard, what is his name?"

"You mean Kevin Diamond," Sarah responded, "He's been with us for about four or five months now. He helps out in the kitchen four days a week in exchange for room and board. Struggling to get back on his feet. His attitude needs some adjustment for sure, but we need his help right now. I hope he hasn't offended you in some way, has he?"

"No, I'm not that easily offended. But I got the feeling the other day when he saw me leaving the office that he had some kind of issue with me, I'm not sure what that's all about. Seems almost like I've seen him somewhere before, but I don't know him."

Amy didn't have to try very hard to persuade Daren to spend Saturday night at her apartment. She had prepared a spaghetti dinner special for him, remembering how it was his favorite kind of food, and nobody could cook spaghetti quite like Amy McBride.

The two of them now realized they had a lot of catching up to do, after having been separated and divorced for as long as they had. This evening had romantic overtones neither could deny – it was a new beginning in a sense, and Daren was especially mindful that if he didn't spoil everything this time around that it just might last, at least for a while.

"If I beat this cancer, Amy... I mean if I get completely cured of it, would you consider marrying me again? We were good together once, and I really believe we could be again."

She didn't answer right away. She looked up at the ceiling for a moment, and then finally into his eyes, "You can't imagine how much I cherish the freedom of being single again, Daren. My life has changed so much since our divorce. But at the same time I've desperately missed the Daren McBride I fell in love with all those years ago, and I see it really as a miracle to be given a second chance – a chance at the kind of happiness we once envisioned. I want that. This could be our last chance ever for something like that, if we can grab hold of it. But it might be a mistake to wait on the cancer. Life is never going to be perfect, and I think we have to be able to understand that. We have to accept the good with the bad in so many ways. Love and commitment aren't meant to be reserved for life's most ideal conditions."

"You didn't seem to have this same mindset during the divorce," he couldn't resist saying, at the risk of spoiling the perfect mood.

"True," her response was fast and she didn't sound at all annoyed by his comment, "but I've had plenty of time to reflect on things since the divorce. I've seen some of my own mistakes, just as you've seen yours."

Daren thought about how her words seemed so well chosen, "You will marry me again then, and risk…?"

"Yes, Daren, I will take the same risk again. Most everything in life has some risk to it. But I finally think I know who you really are now, and what's more is that *you* know who you really are."

"You could become a widow soon, you know."

"That would be my problem then, wouldn't it?"

"I don't even have any life insurance."

"If I were to marry for money it wouldn't be worth it, no matter how much it paid."

"But you could end up being overwhelmed financially with massive hospital bills long after I'm gone. Now that I think about it I'm wondering if it's such a good idea to…"

"Would you stop with all that kind of talk already? Are you trying to talk me out of wanting to be your wife again? You and I both know that some things in life are more important than other things. Let's just try to make it work this time."

"It surprises me Amy that you're still single, or at least not dating someone else right now. I'm sure there must have been plenty of guys pursuing you since we separated, so how were you able to stay in the clear?"

"I've met some decent guys, I can't deny that. But none of them have been able to steal my heart away from you. It's important to me that you understand that fact and that you value it – that you don't take it for granted this time."

"I'm flattered and I do value it. I don't take anything for granted anymore. When would you think a good time for us to get married again would be?"

"Why don't we sleep on that and decide maybe

tomorrow?"

"Fair enough. But I want you to promise me one thing, Amy."

"Again? You already made me agree to it, remember? I promise that I will do everything in my power to bring you up to the lake when the time comes."

He shook his head, "I'm not talking about that right now. I want your word on it that if this cancer beats me – and I'm not saying that I think it will – you know I will fight it 'til the end and I do plan on winning this fight, but if what Dr. Richards told me about it turns out to be true and I don't make it to see next Christmas, that you'll get on with your life and that you won't go out of your way to spend the rest of your life alone. I want you to find new happiness if you can."

"What are you saying, Daren? Are you saying that you'd want me to find someone *else* to get involved with - that you'd actually want me to fall in love with another man?"

"All I'm saying is that I want you to keep living your life, even after I'm gone, because life has to go on for the living. Having this cancer sure has forced me to think about a lot of things differently than I ever did before. Anyway, just please promise me that you'll always be open minded about finding happiness again, and that when my time comes you will allow yourself to let me go, okay?"

"Okay, I promise you that if it makes you feel better. But right now I just want to focus on right now."

"And so do I."

Daren woke up Sunday morning with a strange pain

throughout his upper body. One minute it felt like it was worse in his stomach than anywhere else, and the next minute it seemed to be centered in his chest. He didn't want to say anything to Amy about it while she was getting ready for work. There would be no benefit in her concerning herself with his health while she was at her job, knowing full well she would if she knew how he was feeling.

He managed not to mention anything to her about the pain, but it was becoming excruciating, and she suspected something was wrong by the tense look in his eyes.

"Are you feeling all right today, my love?" she inquired with that worried tone in her voice that he always recognized when he heard it.

"Well enough to knock on some doors I believe," he said. "Once I get out there and start walking in the fresh air and everything, I should be just fine."

"You don't exactly look 'just fine'. I'll ask Mr. Tillman if he'll let me clock out early – maybe an hour or two before my shift ends if we're not too busy, and I'll come home and take care of you tonight, if you don't mind spending another night over. I can make that potato soup you always liked, then you could take a warm bath, and after that I'll give you a massage. On my way home I could rent a movie. That might get your mind off your discomfort for a little while, anyway. Which movie do you want to watch?"

"Oh, I don't really care. How about you pick out one you want to see this time? I especially like your idea of the massage. If that doesn't make me feel like a brand-new man, then nothing will. I think you missed your calling in life, Amy. You'd have made a great nurse."

After she left for work he started coughing, and this time his coughing fit didn't stop in five minutes. It persisted longer, and it progressed into nausea. He found himself already headed for the bathroom when he felt the urge to vomit, and he reached the toilet just in time to avoid making a mess.

It was not encouraging to see the blood in the toilet bowl. And to Daren it looked like an awful lot of blood. When he was finally confident he had concluded his unpleasant business at the toilet, he pulled himself up to the sink and splashed some water in his face, and then he brushed his teeth and gargled with mouthwash he found in the medicine cabinet. He noticed in the mirror how bloodshot his eyes were, and his head started aching. He now realized that this was going to be a very long day for him.

In spite of his almost incapacitating condition he managed to force himself out of Amy's apartment and into a nearby neighborhood to knock on some doors. He heard a car that sounded like its engine needed a tune-up, pull up to the curb and park maybe fifty feet behind him, and then the sound of the car door opening and closing followed by sounds of a barking dog in a nearby yard, but his mind was too focused on his task at hand for his attention to be diverted by these kinds of common background noises.

He made his way up the front steps of the first house at his end of the street and rang the doorbell three separate times. It was the same as with most of them – nobody answered the door. As he was walking away and back down the steps he caught a glimpse of someone's silhouette out of the corner of his eye – someone wearing a hooded gray sweater walking on the sidewalk in his direction.

The image didn't register in his mind as particularly unusual until after he had turned away to continue toward the next house. But then all of a sudden as he reached the front porch it struck him as odd. Someone wearing a sweater with a hood over his head when the sun was shining and the morning's weather was comfortable – maybe around sixty degrees, with no wind or breeze to stir the air. He stopped in his tracks and turned around, but now there was nobody in sight.

"Here we go again," he said to himself, thinking about the prophet character he had created previously in his imagination. This image of a mysterious hooded person whose face was hard to see under the hood also had the hallmark of an occurrence from his imagination. His mind had to be playing tricks on him again, he presumed. It must have simply been a symptom of his current physical state, which was now at its worst since he first learned about his cancer.

He decided to ignore the whole thing and continue with his fundraising effort. The last thing he needed right now were more distractions. As it was he knew he would be lucky just to be able to stay on his feet for even a half hour hour of knocking on doors – he was already beginning to feel light headed, and he struggled to avoid another violent coughing fit. He'd have to hold himself together at least until the end of the day, thinking about all of the people living in despair who would be helped if he just managed to keep at it long enough.

A man who answered the door of one of the houses asked Daren why he was even bothering with trying to help the homeless people. "We all choose our own path in this life," the man said, "and many of those homeless people will always remain homeless by choice. Besides, for every one person you help in this world there will be millions of others needing your help who will never receive it. Despite your good intentions, Mister, there will always be poverty in the world."

"Those are the facts as I see them, too, Sir," Daren responded politely, "but since we all make our own choices, I'm choosing to do what I'm doing. I entertain no illusions about wiping out global poverty, but I still feel compelled to help those people who need my help."

When he had reached the far end of the street, which was a dead end street, after having collected only eight dollars in donations by that time, the hooded figure appeared again. Ironically, the only donation Daren had yet collected – the eight dollars -was from that same man who had just expressed his pessimism.

This time Daren's imagination was going wild, and it wasn't at all the way that psychologist had told him it would be. This man with the hood over his head – even though Daren couldn't see his face clearly, looked and sounded awfully real, and when he approached to within about ten feet he showed Daren part of the snub-nosed revolver he held in his sweater pocket. The gun looked plenty real enough. And then the man motioned for Daren to walk toward one end of a tall, solid wooden fence. Daren did exactly as the man persuaded him.

"You'd have done much better to rob me an hour or two later," Daren said, "I've only managed to collect eight dollars so far this morning. That guy six houses down – he told me that he thinks this is a waste of time collecting money for the local homeless shelter. And yet, he gave eight dollars for the cause. But it's still early. After more people get home from church, or finally wake up after their late Saturday night parties, then the collecting should be more productive. But I only have the eight dollars right now."

"I'm not interested in robbing you, Daren, I don't want the money, just revenge," the hooded man informed him as he directed Daren around behind the fence where they would no longer be within view of anyone else. The residential neighborhood on the opposite side was hidden behind a grove of trees, so they were in a fairly secluded field behind a tall wooden fence, hidden well enough that the man felt confident to pull his gun out of the pocket and aim it at Daren. "I'm going to make you beg for your life."

"Who are you, how do you know my name, and why do you want revenge?"

As soon as the man pulled the hood off of his head, Daren recognized him as the same guy he had asked Sarah about.

"Okay," Daren said, nodding, "Now that I can see your face more clearly I know that your name is Kevin Diamond. Sarah Meade from the homeless shelter told me who you are. But what is this grudge you have against me? What's that all about?"

"You just don't remember, do you?"

"You look sort of familiar, but what should I be remembering?"

"Just about four years ago, you came into my restaurant, *Diamond Deli*, and you and I got into an argument. I don't even remember now exactly what we initially started arguing over – I think we were disagreeing about the reasons why food prices were going up or something equally unimportant. But our discussion escalated, and pretty soon we got into a heated argument – exchanged some nasty insults, and when you left the deli you were promising to teach me a lesson. Do you remember that day?"

"Yes, I guess I do remember that day now. Back then I would pick a fight with just about anyone – the mail carrier, my accountant, my insurance agent, even my own mother if she were still alive. I'm not like that anymore, though."

"Well, you taught me that lesson all right. The next thing I knew, that following week I read your scathing letter to the editor in the paper about the deli. You crucified my restaurant with your comments in that editorial."

Daren felt the shame sweep through him like a heat wave. "I do remember," he said sheepishly. "Jeez, I wish I hadn't written what I wrote. I am so sorry."

"Sorry? *Now* you're sorry, sure, now that I've finally caught up with you and have you at gunpoint. Do you want to know what happened after that devastating letter was printed in the paper?

"Well I'll tell you what happened," he continued before Daren could respond, "By then the restaurant had been serving anywhere from about eighty to a hundred and fifty customers a day, doing better and better as people learned about us, and then all of a sudden the numbers dropped off to maybe only fifteen people on a good day, in just a matter of weeks! It didn't take long at all for our negative image to spread throughout the community and the people…

"The people eventually quit coming in. Pretty soon we couldn't pay the payroll and we had to let even our best employees go, and shortly after that we couldn't even pay the rent on the building! In less than two months we had to close our doors, and I filed for bankruptcy. It was the end of the dream I had had since junior high school. I had saved every spare dime from every job I ever worked to get started, and even with that it took me two years after high school to finally find a bank willing to loan on that type of venture for a guy starting out like me. And then I lost it all - everything, all because of one lousy letter to the editor printed in the local newspaper."

"I never had any idea that my vindictiveness could have such a damaging impact on the lives of others. But you've read those typical negative opinions and harsh criticisms in the daily editorial section, haven't you? They're just people ranting about usually nothing very important. I can't imagine any of those peoples' opinions putting businesses out of business. How do you know my letter had anything whatsoever to do with your restaurant failing?"

"Come on, Daren, don't tell me you can't see how your letter sabotaged our deli's reputation. A lot of customers quit coming in after it was printed. What other possible reasons could there be for what happened? We had great employees, great sandwiches, and business was growing before that. This city isn't so big, and your nasty letter made us the talk of the town – in an especially unfavorable way. People here read the paper and too often they believe whatever they read. There is no question in my mind about whether it was the catalyst for killing the business. We might have sustained it better if we'd been longer established, but…"

There was that word again: *catalyst.* It started to make Daren wonder if he wasn't just dreaming this whole encounter.

"You never bothered to sue me for damages."

"Oh, I wanted to all right, believe me I wanted to. But the two different lawyers I spoke to about it both said pretty much the same thing, that it's hard to win a case against someone who presents his criticisms, no matter how devastating, as personal opinions rather than facts. Even if I had sued and won my case, how much could I have expected to get out of you, anyway? Probably not enough to make up my losses."

"So now you'll just shoot me and call it even then, is that the plan?"

"I'll enjoy watching you beg for mercy, and then maybe I'll shoot you, and maybe I won't. But even if I killed you right now we still wouldn't be even. You ruined my career and killed a life-long dream. I wish I could make you experience the same kind of hard times I've suffered over these last four years."

"Look Kevin, I've experienced some of my own hardships lately so I know something about that, but you have to move on. I do regret a lot of the things I've done and the kind of person I was in the past. I am truly sorry I wrote that letter, but I'm a changed man now. I realize that any changes in my life won't compensate you for the hardships I may have caused you, but your grudge against me all this time hasn't hurt me at all. That's hurt only you."

"Well now I can hurt you, Daren, because I have the gun. I've waited a long, long time for this chance to watch you beg for your life. I couldn't believe my eyes when you showed up at the shelter the other day – I've been trying to find you for quite a while now. But this time I promised myself that I wasn't going to let you escape justice. I followed you home from the shelter last night and slept overnight in my car, waiting for just this very moment," he explained as he thumbed back the hammer of the little revolver.

Daren remained calm and in total control of himself despite his ill health, "You've wasted your time, then, because I've got no reason to beg. If you do kill me now you'll actually be saving me from a miserable end that I am dreading. I'm not saying that I'm particularly eager to end my life right now. I still have some things I'd like to finish before I go if it turns out that way, but in a sense you'd be doing me a favor by giving me a quick way out – I had the same idea myself a few months ago. But you're too late about it because I'm already dying with cancer."

The information caught Kevin by surprise, and he didn't know exactly how to respond for a moment. "If I didn't punish you one way or another, then it'd be like I'm letting you get away with what you've done to me."

Daren shook his head, "I don't think anybody ever gets away with anything, ultimately. I'm convinced now that we all reap what we sow. How old are you Kevin?"

"Twenty eight. Why?"

"I would have guessed younger - maybe twenty four or even twenty five, but anyway, you're still very young. Why throw away a potentially long and fruitful future over some past troubles that have nothing at all to do with the present, or at least *shouldn't* have anything to do with the present, and certainly nothing concerning your future? Your future is yours to do with whatever you want. What can anyone possibly ever gain by brooding over something from the past?

"You could go right ahead and put me out of my misery if you don't mind spending the rest of your life with the knowledge of having killed another human being, not to mention running the risk of life in prison for murder if you get caught. You might think you are collecting justice for having been wronged, but I doubt a jury would see it exactly that way. Just know that there's no undoing whatever you do right now. Not ever."

Kevin suddenly looked confused about what to do next. He looked down at the gun in his hand and realized he didn't really want to use it. He had just wanted to make the strongest possible point, and he couldn't think of a more dramatic a way to air his grievances than with a loaded gun. But Daren's words made sense, and he suddenly realized it.

Daren noticed Kevin's hesitation, "You haven't ever seriously contemplated shooting anyone before, have you Kevin?"

"No, I've never had any reason before. This gun was my grandfather's that he always kept in his nightstand until the day he died. I've never shot it before, not even at paper targets. The only thing I know about it is that it has bullets.

"So you can see that I don't know much about guns, and apparently not so much about getting my life back on track, either, or I'd have moved on already. I guess this whole stunt of mine this morning was pretty foolish, but I was just trying to make you see..." as he spoke he was unknowingly squeezing the trigger.

The shot from the little revolver disturbed the morning stillness and startled three small birds that immediately took flight from a nearby locust tree. Kevin looked up in horror from the gun in his hand as Daren dropped his clipboard and slapped his right hand over his left side to cover the bleeding bullet hole. He thought this felt too real for it to be just a dream.

Chapter 12

Sometimes Something Good Comes From Something Bad

◊

"Oh God Almighty, man, I sure have done it now, haven't I? I wasn't *really* planning to shoot you, in spite of my threats. I swear I didn't mean to pull that trigger," Kevin blurted out with panic in his voice.

Visibly stunned, Daren took two steps forward and Kevin could see the terrified look in his eyes. He took another step and stumbled, then immediately kneeled down where he wouldn't have so far to fall when he finally collapsed. Kevin was able to grab him and support him before he fell down.

Kevin's words came out of his mouth like rapid machinegun fire, speaking as if his mind was racing with a string of thoughts, "I don't have a cell phone, so I can't call 911. And I noticed that nobody answered the doors at those last four or five houses you went to, so there's no use in me yelling for help from this spot. I think I can... Yes, I'm pretty sure I can move you to my car and then drive you to the hospital before an ambulance could even reach you here. So that's what I'll do then, I'll just..."

"No," Daren protested, "Just leave me alone and get yourself away from this place before someone sees you here. I think I might lose consciousness. How would you explain all of this to the police if I never woke up? Right now you need to think about your future, Kevin. I know you're not used to doing that lately."

"This isn't the way things were supposed to go," lamented Kevin. "I didn't mean for this to happen, but I *did* pull that trigger."

"I might've done everything you did if I had been in your shoes. But there's no time for contemplating all that right now. I know you didn't pull the trigger on purpose. So please just get going before someone comes around, and there sure could've been someone around who heard that shot. You'd also be wise to pull that hood over your head so it's harder to see your face clearly if anyone notices you. But try not to draw any attention to yourself. Just casually walk back to your car and then drive away slowly as if nothing ever happened. Please do it. Go now."

Kevin then stood up, turned around, and sprinted away around the fence and down the sidewalk in the direction of his car, but Daren didn't pass out immediately. He lied down on his back in the tall grass and stared up at the big clear sky over him.

The bullet wound was now making his whole left side feel tight, but surprisingly the wound area didn't seem to hurt quite as bad as much of the rest of his cancer-ravaged insides. He realized that this was probably due to shock. Although he was aware that the wound was bleeding, he had no idea about how much blood he had already lost. He started wondering how long it would take him to die. He didn't expect very long.

And then suddenly he could hear the unmistakable sound of that same old clunker car approaching. It drove up over the curb off the street and past the end of the fence, to within what seemed like only about twenty feet from him. The engine was left running, but Daren could hear Kevin jumping out, opening a door to the back seat, and then running over to where Daren lay in the grass.

He checked for an exit wound on Daren's backside and saw there wasn't one, then quickly planted a 2-inch square sticky bandage directly over the bullet hole to stop further bleeding. He propped Daren upright before lifting him up and moving him to the car and into the back seat where he could lie down. In another instant Daren felt the motion of the car moving quickly in reverse before spinning a fast 180-degree turn, and then it sped away from the scene.

"I think I know the quickest possible route to the hospital," he said. "Won't take us more than just a few minutes, and they'll be able to save you."

"I might not make it. You're risking your whole future, possibly for no good reason."

"You'll make it. Modern medicine is amazing."

The trip to the hospital seemed to take a long time, but Daren realized it was probably only maybe ten minutes or less. When they arrived, emergency personnel were quickly summoned and wasted no time moving him into an operating room where he was given a general anesthetic. There wasn't anything else that he could remember after that.

When he regained consciousness he found himself in a hospital bed all connected up with the intravenous tube and monitoring machines. Breathing was more difficult now than it was before, and he could feel a headache coming on. There wasn't much about his present condition that was at all comfortable for him.

There were two policemen wearing plain clothes in the room who had apparently been waiting for him to awaken so they could ask their questions. The doctor was called when the nurse in the room noticed that he was awake.

"Hello Mr. McBride. Do you feel up to answering just a few questions?" he showed Daren his badge, "I am Detective Reynolds and this is my partner, Detective Garner. Whenever any injury involves a gunshot it has to be investigated."

"Okay. I'll help you with whatever you need."

"First, are you aware that you have been shot, and that is the reason you are here in this hospital? The doctor tells us that he did get the little thirty-two caliber bullet out, and the wound is apparently not life threatening because the bullet miraculously missed all the vital organs."

"Yes, I am aware that I was shot. I remember everything that happened."

"Now second question: do you happen to know who it was who shot you?"

"Yes, I do. It was an accident, of course. You'll need to

make that notation in your report. And this was totally my fault really, because I forgot to give adequate instructions about safely lowering the gun's hammer without causing it to fire. Obviously we should have been training with an empty gun. Kevin is not too familiar with firearms."

"So, this Kevin Diamond we have in custody who brought you to the hospital and who is also our suspected shooter, is he a friend of yours?" the officer asked curiously.

"We've had some disagreements over the past four years and I don't know what he may have told you, but I will say that he is my friend. I know firsthand that he's one of those rare individuals who will instinctively put his own life in jeopardy to save someone else, although he doesn't always use common sense."

"So what happened this morning? How did he shoot you?"

"Kevin needs a bit more training in safe gun handling obviously, like I said, but this morning's accident was my fault. I might've explained about keeping the gun's barrel pointed in a safe direction, but I tend to forget that someone who hasn't ever shot a gun before may not automatically know about something as seemingly fundamental as that."

"So let me get this straight. You were actually teaching him about gun handling when he shot you?"

"It was his grandfather's revolver that he inherited. I guess I should have been thinking more about his experience level, or really his *lack* of experience. This is what I get for making such foolish assumptions."

"Well, we'll leave you alone now so that you can get

some rest. Looks like we don't have reason to charge Mr. Diamond with anything besides discharging a firearm inside city limits, but since it wasn't an intentional act on his part there really wouldn't be much point in that, either. Thank you Mr. McBride for giving us the information we needed. We wish you a speedy recovery."

Amy had gotten permission to leave work early as soon as she received the news that Daren was back in the hospital. By the time she arrived his condition had already begun taking a turn for the worse. She could see that he was in a lot of pain right after the nurse left the room, so she called one of the other nurses to request a stronger painkiller.

"His cancer is already out of remission," said Dr. Richards, returning with the nurse, "and progressing rapidly. That bullet wound has also added complications to his condition, making our job more difficult at this point. I don't think he has much time left, Mrs. McBride. I would say maybe only days now."

"He made me promise not to let him die in the hospital. He wants to go outdoors in a more natural environment. Will the hospital release him to my care in the latter stages?"

She noticed that he had fallen asleep after receiving the latest dose of painkiller.

"It will be best if he signs a consent release form before the time comes. I will say this much though, that if you do move him out of the hospital and into the great outdoors, the two of you will quickly discover just how unpleasant his condition can be. Nature always looks inviting when you're feeling good. I wouldn't recommend it for final-stage cancer patients, however."

"Duly noted, Dr. Richards. Thanks for the reality check. I will try my best to talk him out of it when he wakes up, but he gets these ideas in his head and there's usually no changing his mind.

"This may be a tough question for you to answer, Doctor, but do you think there is any chance at all that he could completely recover at this point?"

"I always hate to destroy peoples' hopes, Amy, but as I noted earlier Daren's illness is in an advanced stage and he is in worse shape than he appears right now. I will prescribe some powerful pain medication to take with him just in case you can't talk him out of leaving the hospital. We'll take good care of him while he's here, and monitor his condition closely. We won't move him back into the emergency room until it becomes absolutely necessary. I expect him to remain in stable condition through the rest of today and probably tonight if our luck holds out. You can stay in here with him as long as you wish."

When Daren awoke he was informed by one of the nurses that there were visitors in the waiting room wanting to see him, and she asked him if he felt up to visiting with anyone else besides Amy, who was still with him in the room.

"I think it would be good for you to see some of these people," Amy suggested, "if you can handle that right now. It would sure mean a lot to them, and I think it would do you some good, too."

"Do you know any of them?" he asked Amy.

She nodded, "Some. Sarah Meade is one. I also know Lisa Price from some meetings we both attended recently.

She's here with her husband, or really her *ex*-husband I should say, and their son. I also saw our old landlord, Mr. Harrington waiting out there, and he's got something he wants to tell you. I don't think I know most of the others. They must be the people you work with at your new job I would guess. I tried to call your old buddy you used to work with, Chad, but he was probably at work. I left a message on his machine."

"How did Mr. Harrington know I was here?"

"I called him and told him. When I ran into him last month he asked me to let him know when I found you, so I called him up a little over an hour ago."

"When I moved out of the house I left him a message that he could keep the deposit, and I moved out a day ahead of the deadline."

"I'm pretty sure he's not here with any kind of complaint this time," she said.

Sarah Meade was the first of the visitors received into the room. She overheard part of their conversation as the nurse directed her into the room.

"Sam Harrington asked me to tell you that he'll try to come back later when he gets an opportunity, and he really does want to talk to you, Daren, but he had to leave just now because he was called back to work at his new job," she said.

"You know Mr. Harrington?" Daren asked, surprised.

"We just met for the first time in the waiting room, maybe twenty minutes ago. We got to talking and when he learned who I am and all about your fundraising project for the shelter, he pledged a generous donation of five hundred dollars. He said it was your rent deposit that you were entitled to but didn't want back. He didn't feel right about keeping it, so he decided to simply donate it to your cause."

Daren grinned as much as his physical pain permitted, "Only a few months ago I wouldn't have believed you if you had told me that about the man. But now I've seen how much people can change when they decide to view the world in a new way."

"I won't stay but just a few minutes," she said, "but I just came by to let you know that a lot of people are thinking about you. Everyone at the shelter is concerned about you. All of us are praying for your full recovery."

The Price family entered the room after Sarah left, and Daren felt encouraged when he noticed how healthy Austin looked. This was the first time he had ever actually seen the boy, and he was aware that he and his parents had just returned from Seattle a few days earlier.

"We owe you our lives, Daren," Lloyd said, "there's no way we'll ever be able to repay you for what you've done for us."

"Just live your lives as though every single day is your last on earth, and that will be plenty good enough," Daren said.

"You'll never know how much you've affected our lives," added Lisa, fighting back her tears.

"I'm pleased to see that your son is looking so well now, considering all that he's been through," Daren remarked.

Austin couldn't resist telling Daren what he wanted to tell him, "The doctors say I'm going to be alright – the leukemia will finally leave me alone now, Mr. McBride. I just wanted to tell you myself that I am grateful to you. I will ask God in my prayers for the doctors to do the same for you, too."

"Thanks, Buddy. I can sure use His help with that," Daren said with sincerity.

"Yep. And the most important thing," Austin added, "I am grateful to you for helping my mom and dad get back together, so that we can be a family again."

"Thought you might also like to know, if I hadn't given you an update about it when we last talked," said Lloyd, "that I'm going to counseling now regularly about my temper, and it's making a huge difference. I've learned how to get control of those anger tendencies, and I haven't been experiencing any of the awful rages lately. I don't take my family's support for granted, either. My perspective about a lot of things has really changed, and none of this would ever have happened if it weren't for you, and that prophet. By the way, when will I ever get to meet that prophet, anyway?"

"I never see that old guy anymore, either. I guess when his purpose with me was fulfilled he didn't need to hang around any longer."

"Well, sure would like to tell him about how our lives have changed since he sent you on those goodwill missions."

"I would say that he already knows," Daren assured him.

Daren's new boss, Lane, together with two of Daren's new co-workers at Mammoth, Keith and Nancy, made up the next small group of visitors to be shown into the room after the Price family left.

"We're eager for you to beat this blasted cancer and come back to work, Daren. The company needs your creativity on some of our upcoming projects. Do they know anything here yet about when you'll be good enough to leave the hospital?"

Amy knew the real answer to that question after what Daren's doctor told her, and it suddenly triggered an emotional nerve inside of her. Rather than shed new tears in the room where Daren or his visitors might notice, she decided to step outside the door without drawing anybody's attention, and take about a dozen steps down the hall where she could cry uncontrollably for a few minutes without creating a scene.

She was well aware that the realization of losing Daren forever would pop into her head more frequently as his last hour drew closer, and that she would want to get a better grip on herself in the amount of time they had left together, for his sake if for no other reason. But she also knew that from time to time it would be too much for her. She would have to try to hide her face from him whenever those unexpected emotional moments arrived rather suddenly.

When she was finished crying she wiped her eyes dry and went back into the room like nothing ever happened. By then they were discussing ideas about a new work project, soliciting his creative input, and Amy sat down in one of the waiting chairs and quietly stared out the hospital room window while they talked. She got pretty deep into her own thoughts.

"Would it be too much to ask you guys to donate ten dollars apiece to the homeless shelter?" Daren asked his visitors, "I'd feel a lot better if you could all do that much."

"That's not too much to ask at all, Daren, if it'll make you feel better," said Lane, "In fact, I'll write a check right now for... How about fifty dollars? I'll write it out right now and leave it with you here if that'll work, or with your wife if she's handling those things for you while you're here."

Amy heard just enough of what Lane said to draw her attention away from the window. She nodded to suggest that she would deliver Lane's check to the shelter for him.

"I can't go quite that much at the moment," Keith said, checking his wallet, "but I've got $26.00 in cash here that I'd be happy to spare for your cause."

"I've got a car payment due this month, and that kind of limits my budget," Nancy said, taking her checkbook and a pen to write with out of her purse, "but I can still give you a check for thirty, anyway."

"You guys are the best! I owe you all dearly for this."

"Just get well right away and come back to work!" Nancy said, tearing her check free from her checkbook and handing it to Amy.

Daren's last visitor for the evening was Kevin Diamond. In a way Daren felt surprised to see him, yet in another way it didn't seem at all surprising. Daren made his best bedridden effort to introduce Kevin and Amy to each other. Nobody in the room could ignore the awkward atmosphere created by his visit, at first.

"Kevin saved me from bleeding to death," he told Amy.

"Actually, my foolish actions are the reason your

husband is in the hospital right now, Mrs. McBride, I so regret having to admit."

"But not the *main* reason," Daren corrected him. "It's the cancer that's eating me up inside, not that little bullet hole. Besides, you never had any intentions of pulling that trigger. That was just an accident.

"By the way, I'm not exactly Amy's husband, just so you know. We are technically divorced at the moment, but I would say that we are nevertheless about as much together now as any married couple has ever been."

"Well anyway, Daren," Kevin said, "thanks for saying whatever you said to the police. They released me without filing any charges. All of this has forced me to re-think almost everything I've been thinking for a long time. I will forever be indebted to you."

"So, is it reasonable to conclude that you're no longer angry over my letter to the editor then?"

Kevin noticed the bewildered look on Amy's face.

"It's a long story, Mrs. McBride, and it's kind of hard to understand, anyway. The bottom line is that I acted like a complete idiot and got your husband, um… *ex*-husband, hurt, and so here we are. I don't know if I can ever fix this mess that I have made."

"Could I ask a giant favor of you, Kevin?" Daren said.

"I probably owe you more than anything you'll ever ask of me, but what is it?"

"I managed to get Amy to promise not to let me die in the hospital. Instead, I want to be where I used to go fishing a lot when I was younger. It's my favorite lake because it's so remote up in the mountains, and it has a lot of natural beauty. It'd be a lot better place to go than in an artificial, sterile environment like this one.

"I don't think I'll be walking very well in my present condition, and this will be really hard for Amy to help me do, just by herself. But if you were able to go along with us… We can take my Ford Bronco, set up a campsite and do some fishing, tell stories around the campfire as the sun goes down, and you know, just breathe in nature."

"You're asking me to help your ex-wife take you out of this hospital, and take you up into the mountains *to die?*"

"Exactly. That's what I want."

Amy shook her head, "I was going to try talking him out of it, but of course I knew I'd be trying in vain."

Kevin contemplated the request for a moment. He looked at Daren, and then he looked at Amy, and then he reluctantly agreed to honor Daren's wish and go along to help them out as was requested of him. He felt an obligation to do it, and Sarah ought to be able to manage the shelter kitchen without him for a couple of days, just as she had been doing before he came along, he told himself.

Chapter 13

Daren's Last Campfire

◊

The Bronco motored its way up the rugged mountain road to the remote lake, transporting Daren, Amy, Kevin, and enough camping gear, fishing tackle, food, and beer to comfortably last them for a period of about two weeks.

It was Tuesday just before Noon when they arrived, and there were no other people at the lake besides them. The only sounds to be heard whenever they weren't talking were just the sounds of birds and an occasional breeze whispering through tree branches. This was now late summer, and the temperature was hot outside of shade.

"How are you holding up at the moment, Daren?" asked Kevin, noticing how pale Daren looked after stepping out of the vehicle to stretch his legs.

"The fresh air sweeping off the lake will help me a lot," he said, also stepping out of the Bronco, though more slowly and not without considerable discomfort, and he wiped the sweat off of his clammy forehead. "So will a cold beer, just as soon as we get that cooler un-packed. What about you two? Wouldn't an ice-cold beer appeal to either of you right now?"

"I'll have one with you in a moment, Daren, after we get that tent set up," Kevin said, looking around for a spacious and relatively level area within easy casting range of the lakeshore.

"I think we should eat a sandwich or something before starting into the beer," Amy suggested. "I packed three different kinds of sandwiches. We should probably eat up the egg salad sandwiches first, only because they'll go bad before the peanut butter, especially in this heat.

"Daren, I think some solid food in your belly will only make you feel better, if you can hold it down. It's been hours since you've eaten anything, and this is about lunchtime, anyway. Food has got to be better than just a can of beer on an empty stomach."

"I really have no appetite at all," he said, "but I suppose I could nibble on one of those sandwiches while I'm sipping on a cold can of beer."

Kevin proceeded to pull the big tent bag out of the vehicle and un-pack its components, "How about right over there?" he asked, pointing toward a sandy beach area near the water not more than thirty yards from the Bronco, partly shaded by two tall pines. "Looks like a good spot to me for our campsite. We can cast our lines in right there, and make a campfire somewhere in front of the tent, and the ground is fairly flat."

Daren nodded. He wanted to help with the setting up of the tent, but at that moment the pain in his chest, side, and back was almost incapacitating, and he felt the desperate urge to just sink into a camp chair and rest. He didn't think he would need to rest for more than just a few minutes. He grabbed a chair out of the back, opened it up in the shade close to where Kevin and Amy started figuring out the tent, and sat himself down, "I should be able to help you two with that in just a minute or two, after I get a little breath of air here."

"Don't you even think about it Daren. It's not worth getting that wound bleeding again. Besides, you're looking pale. Kevin and I will get this thing figured out easily enough," Amy said. "Just give us two more minutes if you can wait that long my love, and I'll put a sandwich and a cold beer in your hands. Right now please just stay put and take it easy if you can do that for me."

Daren paid attention to the way Amy and Kevin worked together as they put up the tent. He noticed how they interacted with each other, although it didn't appear to him that either of them gave any thought to that at all. They focused their full attention on the task at hand until it was done.

It wasn't much more than five or ten minutes until they had the tent all set up and staked down such that the wind couldn't blow it over. It was a large four-man tall dome tent, with a sizeable front porch section. They set it up so that the front porch faced the lake. That way they would be able to sit in their chairs with their fishing poles in hand and their lines in the water, all the while enjoying the shade under the tent's porch.

Once the tent was set up and most of their gear unloaded from the Bronco, Kevin and Amy also sat down with Daren, and the three of them ate egg salad sandwiches and drank cold beer. The breeze drifting in off the little lake made the atmosphere feel like heaven. Daren demonstrated more of an appetite than he knew he had and managed to eat every bite of his sandwich, chasing it down with gulps of beer.

The ride in the Bronco up that road had been hard for Daren, but he didn't want to think about that right now. This place was his idea of paradise, and now that he had arrived he wanted to focus on that. This place was exactly where he wanted to be.

As soon as Amy had finished eating her sandwich she got up and grabbed a fishing pole. Kevin watched her curiously as she fiddled around with the fishing reel and rigged up the line with a hook and a sinker, and he was surprised at how she seemed so eager to try her luck at catching fish.

Daren had learned a lot about Kevin from their conversations during the trip out here, and he was beginning to really like the guy. He had seen a visible change in him – in his whole disposition, just since the shooting accident. Kevin was clearly trying to think more positively about everything now - he was beginning to talk about his future with enthusiasm. He had even mentioned considering opening up a new restaurant.

"Kevin, you didn't completely answer my question while we were in the hospital."

Kevin took a sip of beer and set the can down in the chair's armrest holder, "I guess I forgot already. What exactly was the question again?"

"I wanted to know whether or not you forgive me now for writing that mean spirited letter four years ago. It may not really seem all that important at this point, but it is still important to me to know if you do, before I go to my grave."

"You know," said Kevin, "for a long time I was so completely convinced that there was only one reason why business dried up at the deli. I guess I just wanted someone else to blame for it. Lately, though, I've been able to think of several possible causes for what happened, and I can't understand why I didn't consider them before."

"Such as?"

"Well, that Subway Express that opened right down the street from our place, that was about the same time I started noticing things slowing down for us. Their sandwiches are really popular, and we couldn't touch their prices with what we were doing. I would never admit it at the time, but now I'm pretty sure that they did draw a healthy batch of our customers from us."

"That would seem to make sense," Daren acknowledged.

Kevin nodded, "And then if we factor in what was going on with the local economy four years ago, after the mine closed and everything…

"Anyway, I see now that I was wrong to blame you for what happened with the deli – wrong to place blame anywhere at all. Some things just happen, and that's the way things go sometimes. Some things are probably just meant to be, you know? I can see all of that now. So really, it's *me* who should be asking you how you can forgive me for what I've done to you, because I'm pretty sure that you have forgiven me for it."

"I think we all need forgiveness for the things we do that adversely affect others, because ultimately we're all human and we make mistakes. For me lately that Gospel story in New Testament Scripture has begun to make a lot of sense, where it never used to at all in my mind. I've changed my whole outlook on a lot of things. Some of the things that have happened to me – they're like miracles.

"But I don't think it is forgiveness that I owe you, my friend. It wouldn't be forgiveness in this case. It would be gratitude – gratitude for helping me to open my eyes to some things. When I leave this world my life will have actually had some purpose to it, and a bit more than it would have otherwise had were it not for what happened between you and me, I believe. I don't really know how to explain it, but I hope someday you'll be able to understand what I'm talking about."

"That gives me something to ponder for a long time to come I suppose," Kevin said, unable to think of anything else to say. He suddenly saw an opportunity for changing the subject, "Hey, do you think we bought enough earthworms? It looked like we wiped out that bait shop's whole inventory. Eight cartons of worms sure seems to me like an awful lot, even for three people fishing."

"The fish in this lake are always hungry for worms. That just happens to be the kind of bait they prefer, and I've tried just about everything else here at one time or another. I always hate it whenever the fish are really starting to bite like crazy and then I suddenly run out of worms. It's a long drive back down to that bait shop, and you'd be lucky to dig up very many worms in this sandy soil around here. I've tried it before."

"I see that Amy has already baited her own hook while we were here talking, and look at how far out into the water she cast her line. Did you teach her how to do all of that, Daren?"

Kevin and Daren noticed that Amy had wandered up the beach about fifty yards from the tent, apparently trying to get closer to some lily pads where she expected more fish to be searching for food. They both understood also that Amy probably needed a diversion from the main reason they were here, if only for just a little while.

"She's more of an outdoors kind of girl than she looks," Daren remarked. "We used to do a lot of camping together, and she always enjoyed the experience as much as I ever did."

"Forgive me for asking this, but how on earth did you ever mess things up with her? She has quite a rare mixture of good qualities, at least that's the impression I get from what I've been able to see."

"Because I was a complete fool once, that's how. And your observation hits the nail on the head. She is special in more ways than I can say. I just hope that the next man in her life, whomever that might be, won't make the same mistakes I made. She deserves a lot better."

"She looks like she might be younger than you. I mean, not that you look ancient or anything, but I'm just saying that she looks…"

Daren nodded, "She looks young, I know. And you're

right that she *is* younger than I am. I'm forty-two, and she is, well I guess she will be thirty-four this year. That is right, her birthday will be next month. She'll be thirty-four."

Kevin stood up, tossed his empty beer can on the ground and stomped on it with his boot to flatten it out, then pitched it into the garbage bag over by the Bronco, "I'll go collect up some firewood for tonight's fire, and then how about we rig up our lines and go join Amy? You think you'll feel up to doing some fishing in a little while? You could do it mostly without getting out of the chair, and I'll help you with it."

"I should be able to handle it okay. I'll give it a try, anyway."

Kevin proceeded to scout around within the general vicinity surrounding the camp for standing dead wood suitable for fueling the campfire, and he shortened the longer sticks of wood to keep their size manageable before making a neat stack off to one side of the tent's doorway. He didn't quit his project until he had made a three-foot tall stack of firewood he expected would last all night long.

For the first time in weeks Daren started feeling that nagging desire for a cigarette, but he tried hard to ignore it because he didn't happen to have any cigarettes with him. Before reaching for his rod and reel he grabbed another can of beer out of the cooler and opened it. Even if he didn't have any cigarettes right now, he reminded himself, he still had plenty of beer. He could numb his physical pain somewhat with enough beer he reasoned. They had morphine with them for when the pain eventually became unbearable, but he knew that would be the final stage of things.

By two o'clock the fish started biting aggressively, and the three of them were catching sizeable trout with almost every cast – whenever they managed to get the worms covering the hooks sufficiently that is. About half of the time the fish were able to clean the hooks without getting caught.

Kevin had positioned three large rocks in a triangle close to the water's edge with a hollow between them into which he could securely set his own pole upright with his line in the water while he helped Daren bait and cast his line. By this time Daren was struggling to do much of anything very physical, so Kevin handled all of the line rigging and casting for him. And whenever Daren's line tugged with a trout on the line, Kevin would retrieve the trout Daren reeled in and pull the hook out of the fish's mouth before putting the fish on the stringer.

Kevin also cleaned the batch of fish they'd caught using his sheath knife, leaving the heads on them. He explained that gutted fish never stay on a green stick over the fire without their jawbones for support.

"You seem to be quite a woodsman for a guy who's never handled firearms," remarked Daren.

"I used to go on campouts with my dad a lot when I was younger. Dad usually kept a rifle around camp, but he would never allow me to go anywhere near it. He died before my grandfather did, and that's the only reason I inherited my grandfather's revolver."

"Did you happen to bring that revolver with you out here?"

"I totally forgot to retrieve it from the police after they released me."

"Well, mine's in the Bronco. I may not be up to doing much shooting myself right now, but I could probably talk you through some practical, *safe* shooting techniques, if you're interested. There are probably two boxes of ammo with the gun under the front driver's seat."

"Did you ever teach Amy how to shoot?"

Daren nodded, "She's shot my Smith & Wesson before, but that gun was always a bit much for her. Kept promising to set her up with something lighter for camping, but never got around to it. Maybe it's just as well. She might've been tempted to use it on me a time or two," he joked. "But seriously, if we don't get around to any shooting instruction today, Amy could always help you with that another time if you asked her to."

A little later on the warmth radiating from the evening fire gave Daren comfort, even as he was by then feeling physically quite ill. He had roasted one trout on a green stick over the flames, but at this point he really had no appetite and he ate only two bites of it. It wasn't long until he decided to retire to his sleeping bag on his cot inside the tent, leaving the warmth of the fire and the conversation. Kevin and Amy stayed around the fire and talked for another two hours or more.

Daren was in and out of sleep throughout the night, and he dreamt all sorts of unpleasant dreams whenever he did actually sleep. It was certainly one of the hardest nights that he could ever remember suffering through. He was getting a strong sense now that his life would soon end. He hoped he could at least survive until morning, so that he could see one more sunrise before leaving this world.

By the time the morning sun appeared through the pine branches Kevin and Amy were already up and sipping their coffee by the fire that Kevin finally managed to get burning in spite of the dew-covered firewood. Daren could smell the coffee and the wood smoke, but he lacked the energy needed to get up and join them by the fire.

Daren's mouth felt bone dry and his body felt dehydrated, but even just the thought of drinking any liquid at all almost made him feel nauseous. He could smell the aroma of the coffee drifting into the tent from outside the door, but even that didn't appeal to him right now.

He knew that if he had any energy at all he would force himself up out of his bag and outside by the fire, where he could take in the scenery and visit with Amy and Kevin. But such a simple action now seemed completely unattainable without help, in his present condition.

"Is any coffee still left?" he called from his cot, just to get their attention since he didn't *really* want any coffee.

"Daren, you're finally awake!" Amy yelled, hurrying into the tent to greet him. Kevin followed right behind her.

"I must have been dreaming," Daren said. "I guess I slept in."

"How are you feeling this morning?" Kevin asked.

"I can't get my body to move. I've never exactly experienced anything quite like this before."

"No need to get up. We can carry you on your cot

outside, and you can stay lying down," Kevin said, grabbing one end of the cot and motioning for Amy to grab the other. The two of them picked up the cot with Daren on it, and carried him outside in the light of the morning sun, finally setting it down fairly close to the campfire.

Daren could feel the morning sun's rays on his face, and when he opened his eyes he was in awe of the vast blue sky over him. He was suddenly aware that his senses were more sensitive than they ever seemed to be before.

"Are you able to sit up where you can drink a cup of coffee?" Amy asked.

"Maybe I don't want the coffee after all," he responded, not exactly craving the hot drink the way he normally did each morning, and equally not eager to struggle trying to sit upright.

Amy and Kevin both noticed that Daren looked eerily pale. His face was starting to turn almost a shade of light blue in the sunlight.

"Do you want some medicine for the pain?" she asked him, struggling to hold back her tears.

"No. I won't need it. I don't really feel much of anything now. I know that I don't have much time left now."

"No, Daren, please don't do this right now," she pleaded, no longer able to hold back her tears. "Don't leave me now when I really need you here. Please just keep fighting, keep surviving. You were winning and I really, *really* need you to keep fighting this thing, for me if for no other reason."

"Kevin is here with you, Amy. He's a genuine guy. I've

had a clearer picture of so many things recently, and I am completely confident that he will be the most reliable friend you will ever find.

"And Kevin, please take good care of my Amy for me. She really is that treasure you described to me yesterday. You sure won't want to make any of those same mistakes I made. I know you'll make a better go of everything than I ever did."

For a moment neither Kevin, nor Amy could speak. Amy reached into the side of the sleeping bag and grabbed Daren's hand, and just held it with both of her hands.

It suddenly became much more difficult for Daren to focus on the exact words he wanted to say while he was still able to talk. He could now feel the life beginning to drain from his body.

"People really can change into better people," he said, almost slurring his words, "and they can make a positive impact on other peoples' lives, too, you know that?"

She suddenly saw the blank stare in his eyes, and he no longer appeared to be breathing. A gentle breeze swept over the lake and fluttered her hair into her watering eyes. The only sound she was conscious of was that of a crow cawing in some distant tree, and she could feel Kevin's hand on her shoulder to comfort her.

"Yes, I do know it now," she said. "You showed us all how that is possible."

CPSIA information can be obtained at www.ICGtesting.com
Printed in the USA
269484BV00002B/2/P